FANTASTICALLY TWISTED

THE FAIRY TALES BOOK
of Wickedly Entertaining Stories

Ava May

GOLDHAND
PUBLISHING

The content contained within this book may not be reproduced, duplicated or transmitted without direct written permission from the author or the publisher.

All stories, names, characters, and incidents portrayed in this production are either fictitious or adapted from classic stories in the Public Domain. All original additions, including stories, characters and chapter summaries, are copyrighted and may not be reproduced in any form without written permission from the publisher or author.

© 2023 Goldhand Publishing. All Rights Reserved

ISBN: 978-1-7392991-0-1

Contents

This Will Only Sting a Little   2
A Foreword by the Author

1. The Long Sleep   6
   Inspired by The Sleeping Beauty

2. Boots   18
   Inspired by The Puss in Boots

3. The Summer Queen   30
   Inspired by King Frost

4. The Knotted Locks   57
   Inspired by Rapunzel

5. The Astounding Academy for Interesting Demons   71
   Inspired by The Ugly Duckling

6. Dad's Wrestling Match   82
   Inspired by Little Red Riding Hood

7. The Seven Bros   103
   Inspired by Snow White

8.	The Glass Slipper
Inspired by Cinderella	116
9.	The Sacrifice
Inspired by Aztec Folktale	127
10.	Bad Influence
Inspired by King Midas	152
11.	A Taste for Teeth
Inspired by The Tooth Fairy	170
12.	The Alchemist's Android
Inspired by Rumpelstiltskin	180
Pure Damn Beautiful Sorcery		193

Hey, it's Ava! Thank you for joining me on this journey into the world of magic and adventure.

As a token of my appreciation, I'm thrilled to **gift you an eBook filled with some of my all-time favorite unpublished stories.**

Scan QR the code to claim your GIFT eBook!

Get ready to dive into some *twisted* reads. And don't worry, I have *plenty more stories in store for you*, so stay tuned!

This Will Only Sting a Little

A Foreword by the Author

Sometimes I wonder about fairy tales. Whom did the storytellers of old like Brothers Grimm and Aesop write their stories for? If those old tales were really intended for kids, then our poor ancestors must have been traumatized for life!

Imagine getting those stories unfiltered and unapologetic, thick as blood and with no softening over time. And here we are, the fragile descendants, only getting the watered-down, skimmed versions. Talk about being shortchanged! It's like getting a stale cookie instead of a freshly baked one. Let's demand the full-fat, full-flavored versions of those tales!

Cuts might be painful, but scars are like souvenirs from life's wildest adventures. Each jagged line etched into our skin tells a tale that's begging to be shared.

Scars don't keep their secrets locked up tight - they spill them out like a gossip queen on a coffee date.

We all need a good scar or two, whether we're kids or grown-ups. Who wants a boring, safe story with all the sharp edges blunted by armor and trinkets? Bring on the danger, the thrills, and the lessons learned. We're here for the ride - bumps, bruises, and scars included.

In the original fairy tales there are no supportive, singing bluebirds. The frog prince is not only kissed, but bashed repeatedly against walls by the princess. Beauty's beast does not make it in the end, and there are no anthropomorphic cutlery to grieve him. When the mermaid exchanges her tail for human legs, every step feels like shards of glass needling into the softness of her soles. After Rapunzel's savior heroes his way through myriad obstacles and finally finds her, he decides to leave her in the tower after all. She just wasn't his cup of tea, apparently.

Google it! I'm not making any of this up - yet.

Our ancestral stories are like rebellious teenagers, with a mind of their own and a willingness to break the rules. They don't care about geography or borders, and they certainly don't want to be tamed. But these days, it seems like we want to put them in a straitjacket, lock them up and throw away the key.

Why can't we let them be wild and free, with all their twists and turns? After all, life is messy, and our stories should reflect that. So let's embrace the chaos and celebrate the unruliness of our heritage.

Why do we have to make everything prettier and safer? Why do we love it so much to untwist the twisted?

Fairy tales these days are about as real as unicorns, Bigfoot, or the Loch Ness Monster. These days there are no witches, or spells, or wizards. Princes aren't brave any more and dragons are dinosaurs. Magic is sleight of hand, technology and proven scientific methods. We've become so obsessed with the truth that we've stripped away the fantastical from our stories. It's like we're playing a game of Jenga with our history, carefully removing each piece until it's safe enough for our fragile little minds. But all we're left with are the shadows of what once was. Sure, shadows can't hurt you, but they also can't teach you anything.

Confession time: I'm not your average dentist. Nope, I'm more like the villain from a cheesy horror flick. Instead of fixing teeth, I'm all about giving fairy tales some bite! I take those old stories and inject them with some much-needed oomph. I give them shiny new fangs and plump up their lips. Heck, I'll even give them a slick new tongue and some poisonous saliva. Who said dentists couldn't be fun?

The stories you're about to experience have been upgraded with more twists and turns than a rollercoaster ride. They've been remixed, reanimated, and retwisted for your pleasure.

Some will tickle your taste buds like a sweet treat, while others might leave a bitter aftertaste. But all of them will leave a mark on you, like a tattoo you can't wash off.

Don't be afraid to take a bite.
And don't be afraid to get bitten.
This will only sting *a little*.

1

The Long Sleep

Inspired by The Sleeping Beauty

———⋅◈⋅———

*E*vi, *the last hope of humanity, is spirited away and races toward a new, unblemished beginning. A fresh start that could mean the end of civilization on earth. One special agent is recruited to rescue her, and save the world. If she can overcome the deadly secrets beneath the hull of the cargo ship, the Magdalena, that is.*

Special Agent Whisk forced her way through the airlock door of the Magdalena, because, of course, none of the codes that Intel provided worked. Once inside, she removed her handy pocket welder from her field pack and secured the hole in the hull. Almost immediately, the red flashing lights turned blue and then green.

The Magdalena spoke.

OPTIMAL PRESSURE REACHED.
OPTIMAL OXYGEN LEVEL REACHED.
HUMANOIDS MAY NOW REMOVE BREATHING APPARATUS.

"Don't mind if I do," Whisk said to no one, and took off her helmet. Her hair stuck to her forehead in sweaty clumps. She pushed her nose deep into the collar of her suit, sniffed, and immediately regretted it.

"Weehoo! Someone needs a shower."

It took Whisk three years to reach the Magdalena in her tiny ship. If you want to have a better idea of what the ship looked like, just imagine a coffin with a rocket attached to it. Anyway, the point is, if Whisk hadn't learned to talk to herself, and the subtle joys of her own conversation, she probably would not have survived that trip. And she had to survive.

She had to rescue Evi and take her back to earth.

Whisk looked around the airlock, but couldn't see a door anywhere. "How the hell do I exit this sardine can?" she asked out loud, and then the floor lit up in front of her feet in the shape of an upside-down 'V'. No, not a 'V'. An arrow. She stepped on it, and it disappeared. Another appeared in front of it. She followed the arrows until she came face to face with a blank white wall.

"Open?" she asked.

A seamless door slid open in front of her, and the smell of freshly baked bread accompanied by the sounds of light jazz washed over her.

"Well, that's convenient," she said, and walked into the next room.

Naked, Evi leaned against the cryo chamber. Her head buzzed like a beehive. Thoughts zoomed and whirred past each other, and she found it impossible to focus on one at a time.

The standard questions leaped to mind.

Where was she? How long had she been asleep in the cryo chamber? Who was she?

No, wait, she knows that one. Evi.

She wiped the cryo-goo out of her eyes, and a lump

of the sticky stuff splattered on her bare feet. "Shower. I need a shower," she croaked. The inside of her throat was dry and rough, like the outside of a lizard.

She tried to look around to see where she was supposed to go next. Or to find a shower... or actually, find water of any kind. But it was no use. It would be a while before her eyes could focus again.

WOULD YOU LIKE A SHOWER?

That was the ship's voice. Great. That meant all systems – or at least some – were still online. Evi lifted a stiff thumb in the air and hoped to God that somehow the ship could see it. Speaking was still too painful.

ONE SHOWER COMING UP

She heard something move above her head, and suddenly, heavenly cold water poured on her head. She tilted her head back, opened her mouth, and let that sweet H20 trickle down her parched throat.

Whisk did not understand what she was seeing. This didn't look like a long haul cargo ship. Surely, a cargo ship did not have a smooth jazz cafe on board? Was this even a cargo ship? Intel might have been wrong. Not being right is very on-brand for them, but that having been said... this still didn't make sense.

Two days before Whisk left on her rescue mission, a message was broadcasted to all devices across Earth. Phones blared notifications mid-meeting, tablets suddenly exited mindless games, and televisions stopped in the middle of the good parts of countless soapies. The message sent ripples of fear and hopelessness crashing through the hearts and minds of humanity.

Reap what you sow. The queen is dead. Long live oblivion. Fin.

Was this a proclamation of war? A hacker's sick joke? An eco terrorist? No one knew. But one thing was certain:

Evi, the only hope for humanity, the last fertile woman, had disappeared.

Whisk's earpiece crackled to life immediately after the broadcast.

"*Evi Luna has been taken,*" said the voice in Whisk's ear.

"By whom?" She asked.

"*It's unclear at this stage, but a cargo ship has been spotted leaving the solar system at tremendous speed.*"

"Destination?"

"*Colony Nova.*"

"But, terraformation of that planet won't be completed in at least a millennium! It hasn't even started yet! It's just jungles and rocks and who knows what else! Why would they send her there? Why would anyone want to go there?"

"*Unclear. We do not know for certain that Evi Luna is indeed on this ship, but we have to make sure. You have been selected for this mission.*"

"How do I..."

"*Now, for the bad news.*"

"That was the good news?"

"*The only ship available small enough to leave the atmosphere undetected is not ideally suited for the mission.*"

"In what way?"

"*It will take you three years to catch up with The Magdalena. And it will be very uncomfortable.*"

And here she was, standing in a lush carpeted room with big purple sofas like puffy clouds and deep red walls. After being cramped in that flying matchbox, these couches looked mighty inviting to Special Agent Whisk.

So, she sat down. She let the warm embrace of the feather pillows envelope her. Her body ululated with joy. This was exactly what she needed. What was a few minutes of relaxation before she continued her mission? Evi had been waiting this long. She could nap in her cryo chamber for a little bit longer. Something hovered toward her. A dish, and on it, a silver dome.

She lifted the dome, and immediately her nostrils were bathed in a divine aroma. Fresh, crispy Portuguese rolls. Mussels in a creamy garlic sauce. Hot sauce on the side.

All her favorites.

Evi walked to the ship's bridge, the crisp air of the barren corridors rousing goosebumps on her naked body. The ship had woken her up, so that meant she had to be close to her new home, Colony Nova.

The time had come for humanity to start anew. Completely fresh, without its treacherous history. That's why she decided to leave earth behind and, with the help of the New-novians, commandeer the Magdalena. She wondered how the wretches on Earth had taken the little message she had left them.

Evi smiled at the thought.

When she arrived at the bridge, Ai-Ai was waiting there for her. He was a robot, the Magdalena's pilot and Evi's only companion on Colony Nova.

"Are we there yet?" asked Evi, most of her voice having returned.

"24 *hours till descent,*" replied Ai-Ai in posh British.

"Wonderful," said Evi. "Say, Ai-Ai, do you have any other accents? Something more subtle? I'm not sure if that one's going to work for me."

"*Sorry, Miss Evi, this is what I sound like. No other settings have been downloaded. There was only enough time to prime with software and hardware sets for my two main functions. AI1 and AI2. Artificial Intelligence and Artificial Insemination.*"

Evi sighed. "I guess that will have to do."

"*One more thing, Miss Evi. We seem to have had a breach in the airlock.*"

"What? Are we leaking oxygen?"

"*No, oxygen levels are optimum. The breach seems to have been sealed again, from the inside.*"

"I'll go check it out," said Evi, wondering who the hell was aboard her ship.

"*You'll need this,*" *said Ai-Ai, handing her a pulse gun.*

Whisk wiped her mouth with a napkin. Four plates later, she was bulging out of her spacesuit. "Holy balls! That was amazing!" she said. "Time to get going and save the world."

She pushed her hands down on the velvety material of the couch, and tried to get up. It was more difficult than she expected. She was drowsy, but who wouldn't be after all that food!

ENERGY LEVELS CURRENTLY AT 67%
WHY DON'T YOU HAVE A NAP?

"I really shouldn't," she answered.

JUST FOR A WHILE.
YOU NEED ALL YOUR STRENGTH TO SAVE THE WORLD.

"That is true…" she said, and fell back onto the couch. Her head sunk into a pillow and a silky blanket fell over her body. "Just a few minutes. "DeBussy started playing in her ears.
Her favorite.

Orange arrows lit up on the floor and showed Evi the way. She followed, pulse gun pointed straight ahead. She walked for what felt like miles. and miles. She passed living quarters and kitchens; crew areas, equipment rooms, and massive, fully stocked pantries.
It was a real shame she had to get rid of all of it once she reached her new home. New beginnings are all or

nothing. Otherwise it's not really a new beginning, is it? It's just a ruse. An illusion of rebirth. Ai-Ai awaits the same fate, once he has done his part in helping her repopulate Colony Nova.

The only things – artifacts of a broken past – going with her are Ai-Ai and a repository of diverse DNA sets. The arrows stopped blinking, and she found herself in front of a door with a room log flashing in red.

LIFEFORM DETECTED.
LIFEFORM CAPTURED.

She lowered the pulse gun. There would be no need for that anymore. "Poor sod," she said. "Whomever, or whatever you were." The door to the 4D Holo-Trap slid open and Evi entered. The walls, floors and ceiling of the room were a matrix of gray panels, each an extraordinary piece of equipment that could emulate any sensory input. From touch, to smell. Even taste. Holo-rooms were usually used for training and entertainment, but this one had been modified to be a sophisticated trap. Subduing an enemy by this means was much safer than having artificial weapon-wielding soldiers on board.

Evi scanned the room for its victim, and she almost missed it. In the furthest corner sat a little bundle. As she walked closer, she saw that it was a space suit, and inside it, a humanoid skeleton. On the space suit's chest was a name:

WHISK.

"It's better this way," Evi whispered and stroked the skull. "At least it was a pleasant death."

---

9 MONTHS LATER

Hand-in-hand, Evi and Ai-Ai walk through thick growth of unknown color. His heavy metal feet crush unknown insects. Her fragile toes dig deep into unknown soil. Unknown things scurry away, and others come closer for a better look.

"Welcome home," she says to herself as an explosion ripped through the vacuum outside the planet's atmosphere, and pieces of the Magdalena shoot in myriad directions, entering into new, unknown orbits.

Epilogue: The Lesson Behind the Story

Humanity does not have a great track record. We are an enigma of contradictions. We settle our differences by waging war. We move forward by destroying our planet, our home. It seems in all of us, there is a little bit of evil tucked away. But, were we created like this, or did we become this? Can we truly erase our history and start fresh somewhere new? The choice is ours.

2

Boots

Inspired by The Puss in Boots

---※---

At an elderly care facility, members of the exclusive Oaky Shades backgammon group are mysteriously vanishing one after the other. Granny Agatha and her murderous feline companion are the only ones who know to the truth behind the abductions, and it appears that at least one of them is willing to spill the beans.

No one believed Agatha. Not a single word that came out of her ancient, wrinkly lips.

They didn't believe her when she told them about the sunflowers in her old garden that used to bloom straight through winter. They didn't believe her when she told them somebody stole her favorite garden gnome's fishing pole. And they certainly did not believe her when she told them that the body they had dug up behind the bird bath was news to her, as well.

So why would she even waste her breath by trying to tell them that the real culprit was in fact Boots?

Boots, a black Persian cat with white paws, was Agatha's whole life, or what she had left of it at ninety. He was there on her brittle body when she woke up at 4 am each morning. He was there on the edge of the bath when she washed off each day's drama with lukewarm water. He was there in the garden, watching snails squirm in agony, as Agatha showered them in salt. He even went shopping with her and accompanied her to Saturday backgammon club in Jemima's room.

Jemima lived two rooms down from Agatha in the Oaky Shades retirement home and, apart from Agatha, she was the last remaining backgammon lady. The other four or five suddenly started dropping like flies the previous year.

When Trish, Agatha's only granddaughter, arrived at

Oaky Shades for her monthly visit, she found Agatha and Jemima scuttling through the old age home's echoey halls. It was apparent to Trish that they were on some kind of mission. She tried to keep up with them as they sporadically darted in and out of rooms. They were slow, but agile.

"Gran!" Trish shouted from behind them.

"Can't talk now, my baby," she said without stopping or looking back. "We're running an important errand!"

"Gran! Please, slow down. I can't stay long. I need to go to extra math classes in an hour. If I don't show up for that again, my mom, your daughter, will literally kill me!"

Trish wasn't crazy about these monthly visits. The whole place smelled like old socks, soup, and sanitizer. And Gran never wanted to talk about anything she wanted to talk about. She didn't even know what TikTok was, even though Trish tried to explain it to her a gazillion times. And she had a sneaky suspicion that her Gran hadn't even heard about Facebook. Facebook! The place where old people go to die! All Agatha wanted to talk about was chrysanthemums and bougainvilleas, and dumb, ugly garden gnomes.

"If you die, you die," said Jemima in a hoarse, Darth-Vader-esque voice. "This is more important than solving for x. We're recruiting members for our backgammon club."

They were still power walking, slippers flip-flopping on the sticky linoleum floors.

"All the others are dead," said Agatha.

"Murdered, you mean," Jemima corrected her.

Murdered? *These fossils are losing it*, thought Trish, and she stopped.

"I'll wait for you in your room, Gran," Trish shouted after them as they disappeared around a corner. She shook her head in exasperation.

When she reached Agatha's room, her worst enemy was, as always, waiting for her there on the bed.

He was splayed out on the army green quilt, washing his private parts.

"I hate you, Boots," she said, but the cat did not even look up. "No one believes me, but I know. I know you're evil."

She absentmindedly touched the place on her arm where Boots had sunk his fangs into her skin two months ago. He would not let go. It took a trip to the emergency room with the vicious cat attached to separate them. And all because she took a biscuit from Gran's plate. Mom wanted the evil piece of shit put down, but Gran would not hear about it. Which is the reason she planted the camera in Gran's room in the first place. She wanted to catch Boots in the act, next time he did something diabolical.

Trish walked to the window to look at the familiar

gnome-riddled garden below, but today the view from Gran's room was quite different than usual. Today, there were actual people down there. In uniform. And there was a police car with red-blue rotating lights. And a perimeter of sunny yellow tape that said DO NOT CROSS.

One of the police officers, a fat one, struggled up from his knees with visible effort and shouted something inaudible. He pointed toward the hole he had been digging. Trish pressed her face against the window for a better look, and the frosty chill of winter burrowed through her nostrils and into her brain. She tried not to breathe. For once, something interesting was happening at Oaky Shades and she was not about to let the vapor cloud up the window and obscure her view. What was happening down there. What did they find?

"All done," shouted Agatha, and Trish nearly jumped out of her moccasins. "Harold is joining the club."

"What the hell, Gran? Do you want me to be the first teenager to die of a heart attack in an old age home?"

"Firstly, it's a boujee retirement destination. It says so on the pamphlets. And secondly, what are you looking at?" Gran huddled in next to her and followed her eyes. "Oh, lovely. I wonder if they found Denise!"

"Denise?"

"Yes, they've been looking for her since they found

Maggie behind the bird bath. Dead as a doorknob. Her throat slashed with something sharp and thin."

Boots stretched out on the bed, flexing his dirty, hooked claws.

"Her throat slashed?" Trish gasped and looked at her gran with eyes the size of dinner plates.

"Tea?" Gran asked and noticed the expression on Trish's face. "Oh don't look at me like that! It wasn't me," she snorted. "It was Boots."

"Boots?"

Boots meowed. It sounded like the meow of someone devious trying to look innocent.

"But it's not his fault, the poor old fluffybutt. He was just trying to protect me. People warned me I should stop dressing him in clothes. They said he would start to think he was human. And when human intuition mixes with brutal animal instinct, the results are not good. Just ask Maggie and, oh yes, I'd notice that perm anywhere, even covered in mud. That's definitely Denise."

Two police officers, a ginger man and a tall lady, were now trying to put a body into a black bag, but they were not winning. Trish wanted to look away, but she couldn't. The spectacle reminded her of the time she tried to put her tent back into its bag after a miserable camping weekend with her dad. It just would not fit.

"I always told Denise to be careful with what she put in her body. Eight macaroons a day, I tell you. Eight!"

"Gran, why would Boots kill these poor old people?" Trish humored her gran. She believed Boots was indeed the essence of evil, but how could a cat murder human beings? Was that even possible? She looked deep into Boots' yellow eyes and tried to figure out what he might be thinking.

"You see, Boots is very attached to me. Very, very attached," Gran said, and switched on the kettle. "It all started when he started coming to our backgammon games. He's our mascot, you know. Anyway, I used to be the champion. I won every week! Can you believe that?"

"I can believe that, Gran," Trish said, and she could. Her gran was spectacular at everything she did.

"But I've been getting older much quicker the last few months. My mind and my eyes are starting to turn on me." Gran made us two cups of tea, and poured some in a bowl for the alleged murderer, who was purring on the bed. Boots meowed in appreciation.

Butter wouldn't melt in that little turd's mouth, Trish thought.

"So, after a winning streak of weeks, I started losing. And Boots, he's a smart little fellow, you know. He started noticing that I did not take it well," Gran continued. "I'm not good at losing."

"Yeah, I remember the time you flipped over the monopoly board when mom bought Boardwalk, before you could," Trish said.

"Don't remind me about that day! Anyway, at first Boots only attacked their shins and calves, and sometimes their bare feet, if they were so brave to walk barefoot around them. But later, members of the club started disappearing."

Trish took a sip of the excruciatingly sweet tea and nodded eagerly, to show her gran that she was invested in the story.

"The rest of us didn't think much of it at first. I mean, people get up and walk out of this place all the time. Dementia is real! But then I started noticing a pattern."

Trish leaned in closer. "A pattern?"

"Yes, a pattern. Everytime, one of our backgammon club members disappeared, it was the day after they had won!"

"Gran, how could there be a pattern? Only two people disappeared, right?"

"No, five."

"What?"

"Five people disappeared. Bert, Miranda, and Maude are still missing. But it looks like the police are on a roll down there. They might find them today! It shouldn't be too hard. Boots is a killer, but he's not a digger. The graves must be very shallow."

"But how does he get the bodies to the garden?" Trish asked.

"Oh, he's a sly one," Gran says, stroking his tail. "He lures them to the garden. All the residents here know that when Boots rubs against their legs, he wants to go for a poop in the garden. And honestly, the other people love taking him for walks. It gives their lives a bit of purpose."

"So, he lures them to the garden, slits their throats with his claws, and then?"

"Well, he's always busy digging holes down there. He's like that. So, I'll bet he waits till they're standing in the right spot, jumps up, slits their throats, and then after they have collapsed into one of the hole's he's dug, he covers them with dirt."

"Just like he would cover one of his poops."

"Exactly, "says Gran, "Would you please excuse me? I need to go to the little girl's room."

"Sure thing, Gran," Trish said, and as soon as Gran closed the bathroom door, she jumped up and rushed toward the bookcase.

She browsed through the books and random objects until she found it right where she had left it. Between the ceramic statue of a pug and a battered copy of *Murder on the Orient Express*, hidden behind a dried out potted cactus, stood her camera on its little tripod.

Quickly, she grabbed it and opened the panel on the side that covered the memory card slot. Finally, she'll have proof that Boots isn't only insane, he's also a serial killer! She pressed the button next to the slot, but nothing happened. The 1TB memory card, which she had 'borrowed' from her mom, was supposed to pop out. She held the camera up to the light and peered into the slot. Maybe it was stuck in there? But no, it was empty. What the hell? Had she forgotten to put the card in the camera?

She had to go home immediately. If she had been stupid enough to do that, the memory card would still be in her drawer at home. That memory card was hella expensive. And if it was gone, her mother would kill her. Twice! She had to know.

But also, if it really was gone... who would have taken it? Gran doesn't even know how to use the convection oven dad bought her for Christmas.

She threw the camera haphazardly into her backpack and rapped on the bathroom door.

"Gran," she yelled through the thin door.

"Almost done," her gran yelled back.

"Never mind that, I need to run, or I'll be late!"

"Love you!" yelled Agatha, but her granddaughter had already left.

Moments later, Agatha emerged from the bathroom with a plastic shopping bag in her hand. Boots patted at it playfully.

"No, no. You can't play with that. These are Gran's toys."

Jemima entered the room, pointed at the bag and asked: "Is everything in there?"

"I think so," said Agatha.

"Are you sure that camera saw it happen?" asked Jemima.

"Bert didn't want to go to the garden, so…" Granny trailed off, and shooed Boots away from the quilt he had been lounging on. Then, she lifted the quilt to reveal a dark stain on the flowery pink bedding.

"Oh, that's not good," said Jemima. "I'll take care of that later. For now, I'll get rid of all this." Jemima looked in the bag and took inventory of the contents.

1 x Memory card.

1 x Pencil sharpener.

1 x Sharpened knitting needle

"It's all here," Jemima confirmed.

Agatha smiled a warm, friendly grandmotherly smile, and thought to herself, "*Granny Agatha never loses.*"

Epilogue: The Lesson Behind the Story

Some people will go to any lengths to win, even if that means cheating. And in some cases, even if it means killing, so always watch your back. Over-competitiveness can be dangerous. Remember, sports are only sports, and games are just games. But not to everyone...

3

The Summer Queen

Inspired by King Frost

In a cold and icy land, where magic reigned, a cold-hearted queen controls the remains... Will the sun ever rise again? A young girl named Hazel is about to rewrite the fate of the land. It is time for the seasons to change.

Nestled in the heart of a dense forest, Frosthold was a dark and gloomy village surrounded by tall, snow-capped mountains. At the eastern edge of the village, there was a grand castle made of ice—the home of the Snow Queen, who ruled the villagers with a cold and merciless hand. The villagers feared and respected her because she protected them from the cold winters and the dense forests surrounding the village. Or so she said.

The Snow Queen was the only person who knew magic in a land that had lost its magic ages ago. The Snow Queen was powerful, but she rarely concerned herself with the villagers. And life went on in perpetual winter. The sunlight was pale and weak whenever it reached the ground. And the sun remained a shadow of itself even during the day. The village was gloomy because villagers worked hard to put food on their tables and stay warm.

That night, the village was a little less gloomy with the arrival of Christmas. It was an occasion of celebration like no other in the village. The wooden houses were lit with candles and lanterns until they glowed like fireflies. The smoke coming from the chimney brought with it inviting smells of roasted turkey and apple cider. The snow that covered everything like a thick blanket was shoveled off streets until the cobblestone beneath became visible. The street lamps, which had remained unkindled for the last few months, were rekindled.

Yuri saw a daughter and her father building a snowman in the yard of a brightly lit house. The mother stood in the doorway and smiled, looking at the scene with amusement. The light coming from the house illuminated her figure as though she was an angel showering her blessing upon her kid and her husband. She reminded Yuri of his deceased wife—a kind and comely woman who loved everybody and always had a smile. Thinking of her made him feel guilty for not bringing his late wife's daughter, Hazel. There was to be a celebration in the village square, and she had been excited to be a part of it. But his present wife, Anastasia, had refused. "Oh! Forgive me, my dear child. You cannot come with us. What if a burglar stole Emily's clothes and jewelry with nobody in the house to guard them? With those brutish arms of yours, I bet you can bring down ten burglars." Anastasia had made the sweet girl giddy with anticipation and stomped on her longings with a cruel trick.

Yuri had stood up, slamming his fist on the kitchen table. He had had enough of Anastasia's cruel acts and remarks, but the swan-like hands of Hazel on his shoulders and the word of God in his memories had stopped him from ruining the night.

Yuri didn't want to acknowledge it, but it was also the fear of becoming lonely once again that had stopped him. His hair had turned gray, and his face had lost its suppleness. After a hard day of work, his body ached more than it used to. Besides, if he fought, he would accomplish nothing. Anastasia would become crueler and meaner to Hazel. So, he swallowed his anger and left the house, leaving her first daughter alone on Christmas.

"Forgive me, Yuri. You know I love you and Hazel," said Anastasia, which pulled Yuri out of his thoughts. "She is a good girl. Hazel is, but charmless. She must learn to work and sacrifice, or her life will be ruined after marriage. Why! The world will blame me if I did not teach her those values. You know the cruel things that are said about stepmothers."

As Yuri, Anastasia, and Emily were leaving their house for the Christmas celebration, Anastasia ordered Hazel to prepare the feast. "Hazel, would you be so nice to prepare the turkey and cook roast potatoes, gravy, and cranberry sauce? And, yes, those lemon cakes as well. Emily loves them, don't you, Emily?"

Emily joined in at that, "And don't overcook it this time."

Yuri grunted but said nothing. Even now, he walked silently towards the village square for the Christmas celebration as his wife tried to persuade him. All this cruelty overwhelmed Yuri, but he was giddy with anticipation because he had secretly bought a gift for Hazel.

Hazel was nothing like her stepmother had described. She was a beautiful girl of sixteen with jet-black hair and big hazel eyes. Inside the kitchen of her home, she was sitting on the chair with her head on the table, thinking about the festivities outside. At first, she sobbed while feeling bad about herself, but she gathered herself and worked, crying. Working helped her keep her mind off things. So, she worked whenever anything troubled her.

Hazel was not naïve. She knew what had happened. Her mother had deliberately built her hopes up only to tear them down. Since morning, Hazel had cleaned the house, washed the clothes with freezing water, and prepared the feast. Like every other day, her stepmother and her sister sat around the kitchen table gossiping and suggesting things for her to do. Hazel hated washing clothes because her stepmother did not allow her to use hot water. But Hazel loved cooking, and tonight, she enjoyed lighting the house with candles and lanterns.

If someone were to stand outside Hazel's house, they would find it glowing like a sprightly firefly against the sweeping darkness of the winter. Hazel prepared the candles by adding fragrance oil to the melted wax and pouring the mixture into a mold. She used a variety of fragrance oils. The result was that her house smelled like a garden.

In the evening, after she had done all the work, she bathed and donned her sister's old gown, which was a tad bit big for her. It also had a hole, which she had expertly patched. Her father had looked at her and called her the most beautiful girl in Frosthold. Her sister did not like that at all. She had remarked that Hazel looked like a monkey in a dress. Her stepmother had laughed loudly at that.

"A monkey that will go to the village square," Hazel had replied.

"No, you will not," Emily had shot back. Emily had gotten her wish. When everyone left, Hazel had torn the gown off her body and donned her old drabs, feeling sorry for herself.

When she started working, she forgot about her woes. She had prepared the turkey, the potatoes, the gravy, and a few other things her father and stepmother liked. They were a surprise for them. She always planned for that. She had prepared trout for her mother and a glass of mulled wine for her father. After what her stepmother had done to her, she wanted to throw away the trout or feed it to the animals that came to her at night, but that would have been cruel and unkind. Her father had told her that Hazel's birth mother was the kindest woman of Frosthold. Hazel wanted to be like her.

Hazel had prepared everything. She was just waiting for the lemon cakes. *Oh, no*, she thought and rushed to the oven. She put out the fire and removed the lemon cakes. She felt relieved. They looked perfectly fine to her. That was how she liked them, but not her sister. There was nothing to be done, so she resigned herself to the cruel remarks she would get. She had learned patience from her father. "Accept things outside of your control," Yuri once told her. "You will be happier."

Hazel wondered if her father had said the same thing to her stepsister. The girl accepted nothing. She would find fault in the moon. Hazel's lemon cakes were a measly thing. She knew her stepsister would be outside complaining about things—about the cold, about her dress, or about the villagers. The only thing that shut her up was when Hazel mentioned King Frost, a monster that lived inside the forest. *Maybe that is what I will do when Emily opens her mouth*, Hazel thought to herself and chuckled.

Hazel placed some of the prepared food in a food basket and covered it with a thick cloth to protect it from the cold weather. The food smelled very compelling, but she would eat with her family. She covered herself up in a warm woolen coat and scarf and trudged through the snow with a basket of food in her arms. Her breath came out in visible clouds as she walked, her boots crunching through the snow.

Hazel was on her way to visit her elderly neighbor. He was a grumpy old man, tough on the outside and soft on the inside. He treated people the way they treated him. He was very nice to Hazel and her father. But he was very mean to her stepmother and Emily. In his old age, he still worked to gather wood and food. Hazel's father helped him with the firewood often, and Hazel sneaked leftovers for him when she prepared something nice. Her stepmother had caught her only one time, but that was because she never entered the kitchen except to eat or find some fault.

As she approached her neighbor's small cottage, Hazel could see the smoke from the chimney, a sign that at least the fire was keeping the place warm. She knocked on the door, and the old man, Mr. Jenkins, who looked thin and frail opened it.

"Hazel, what a lovely surprise," Mr. Jenkins said.

"I wanted to bring you some food I prepared for Christmas."

"Come inside, sweet child. Spend a few minutes with this lonely old man."

Hazel followed the old man into the dark cottage where Christmas was nowhere to be found. There were no presents, feast, or light except the fire inside the hearth. Mr. Jerkins pulled the boiling kettle from the hearth, "Sit down, Child. Don't punish those legs of yours. God knows how hard you work all day."

Hazel placed the food basket on the rackety table, which had two white cups and two white plates sitting on it. Mr. Jerkins brought the kettle to the table with shaky hands.

"Let me help you, Mr. Jerkins," said Hazel as she took the kettle from the old man's hands.

"It was kind of you to bring me food. I like your cooking very much," said Mr. Jerkins as he sat down slowly. "I was looking forward to it."

At that, Hazel looked at the old man. "Oh, yes," said the old man. "I knew you would come. You are just like your mother. Just as beautiful and just as kind. She couldn't handle anyone sitting alone in a corner. She had to bring them in the warm company of others. No one felt excluded when your mother was around."

Hazel poured the hot tea from the kettle into one cup. "Pour one for yourself, Child. I had two cups laid out for me and you."

Hazel poured tea for herself and said, looking at the

two plates, "I cannot break my fast here, Mr. Jerkins. I must eat with my family." But looking at the old man, she felt bad. Sure, breaking fast with your family was the right thing to do, but it was nicer to make a lonely person feel loved. That was what her mother would have done. *Mr. Jerkins must feel so lonely*, she thought. She had her family, but Mr. Jerkins had no one. Nobody knew much about Mr. Jerkins' family. He had been living here since he was fairly old. And whenever Hazel asked him about them, he would get a forgetful look on his face. It was as if he had forgotten about them. Hazel knew people often forget memories about terrible things that happened to them. But what Hazel did not know was that it was magic that made the old man forgetful.

"I shall eat some lemon cakes with you," said Hazel as she sipped her tea. "I know you like them very much."

"Oh, yes. Yes, I do. But I like your company even better, Little Dove. I wish I had something to give you for Christmas."

The old man and the young girl broke their fast on lemon cakes and were very glad for each other's company. They talked about many things, but Hazel, above all, loved talking about her birth mother. Hazel perked up anytime when her mother was mentioned. "I wish I could see and talk to her just one time."

"I wish the same thing, my child. And I assure you,

so do your father and everyone else in the village who knew her."

Both avoided mentioning Anastasia and Emily because that would propel Mr. Jerkins into a rant about them, ruining the peaceful Christmas night. Instead, they talked of things warm and kind until Hazel remembered her stepmother. A chill went through her body.

"I must take my leave, Mr. Jerkins," said Hazel. "It was so very nice to meet you."

"Give me a moment, Child. I think I have something to give you. It was possessed by my son, or at least I think so." He fished inside his pocket with a concerned look. And he pulled out a red, transparent stone. Mr. Jerkins turned the stone in his hand, frowning. It was as if he was seeing the stone for the first time.

"Here you go, Child," he said as he gave her the stone from across the table. The red stone was warm to the touch and heavier than she could have guessed. *It was a peculiar thing to give,* thought Hazel, but she was grateful and took it in kindness.

"Thank you, Mr. Jerkins," said Hazel as she took the gift and rushed off, announcing a hasty goodbye to the old man.

When Hazel stepped outside, she felt different. She saw the forest extending to both sides. She felt drawn to the forest. *How peculiar*, she noted. She had never been drawn to the forest. She was always a little scared of it. It was not the animals that scared her. Late at night, many animals came to her house from the forest. She had given them food and drink, and she had nursed their wounds before. She guessed they always came late at night because they were scared of people. It started three years ago with an owl. And then came other animals. Wolves, bears, and fawns. But she had kept it a secret lest they call her a witch.

Hazel forced herself to look away from the forest and hurried to her house. She left the torn gown lying on the ground. Her stepmother would use that against her and the fact that she had left the house. When she neared her house, she saw her little friend, Frostwing, perched on top of the yard's gate. Frostwing beat her wings when she saw Hazel.

"Forgive me, Frostie. I am in a hurry. I will return to you."

The owl nodded its head as if she knew what had been said, and Hazel rushed off. Yellow light streamed out of the door's glass. She opened the door, and she saw ... No one. She sighed with relief. She picked up the gown from the floor and inspected it. It's patchable. She climbed the stairs and into the attic. She opened her trunk and shoved the gown inside it. *Here you go.*

She heard the distant voice of her stepmother and stepsister. She hurried back down. As Anastasia removed her scarf and coat, she complained about rude behavior in the village square. "That serving girl! Who does she think she is." Mentioning a serving girl reminded Anastasia of her stepdaughter. She darted her head and saw Hazel coming from upstairs. "Are you sure you were not rummaging amongst Emily's things," said Anastasia, looking at Hazel suspiciously. "And what happened to Emily's gown?"

"I put it inside my chest, Mother. It was itchy." Anastasia looked at the girl up and down. Surely, removing her dress was an act of contempt against her. But seeing her stepdaughter back in those drabs pleased her. She could not help but smile. "And have you prepared the food?"

"Yes, Mother," said Hazel.

"Then why are you standing here like a goat? Emily is hungry."

Hazel went to work to lay down the food on the table, listening to the bickering of her stepmother and sister. Emily complained about the cold and the fact that she had to stand in line with others for apple cider. "But how grand was the Christmas tree?" said her stepmother loudly. "How magical. Little fairies flew everywhere. And the tree changed color. It went from green to purple to violet. Vendors sold warm drinks and treats. The smell of gingerbread cookies and hot cocoa filled the air, and the fireworks," exclaimed her mother as Hazel placed a plate in front of her. "Oh, how I wish you would have seen it, Hazel. It created a pink ice castle in the sky. I am certain we saw magic."

It was indeed magic. Snow Queen held the monopoly for magic and made sure everyone knew it. It was a display of power for her. She had also sent an army of soldiers and wizards. A few with great magical potential within them had been arrested. Hazel was lucky she didn't go because they would have arrested her immediately.

When the feast was laid, everyone sat down, and Yuri said a prayer, thanking God for providing food on their table. Hazel kept peeking at others. To see if her father liked the food and to detect displeasure on her stepmother's and stepsister's faces. To her delight, no one complained. And her father thanked her for the wine, saying, "Thank you, Hazel, for the wine. Just what I needed after our little excursion. And the trout is wonderful as well," he said with a smile. "Your mother seems like she enjoys it." Anastasia coughed at that. "And the lemon cakes. They are delicious as well," said Yuri, looking at her daughter.

"Ma, can I take Hazel to cook lemon cakes for me

after I am married?"

"No, Emily, I need her to cook wonderful trout for me," said Anastasia.

Yuri put his fork down and said, "I am touched by the love you both have for my daughter, but she will marry a handsome and kind man."

Emily snickered at that and said while chewing, "Father, you should talk to Bubba. He and Hazel would make a fine couple indeed."

Anastasia laughed loudly. "I saw him at the village square, drooling."

Yuri had finished eating. He was wiping his hand on a towel. "A few days ago, Lieutenant Janos' son, Arthur, came to our shop. And let me tell you. He seemed infatuated with Hazel." Hazel shot a look at her sister. Her sister's mouth lay open, food clinging at the edges. Emily looked like Bubba in a gown.

"You are lying, Father," Emily shot back at her father. But she knew inside her that her father was telling the truth. Emily was unlike her mother, who was blinded by her hatred of Hazel's mother (then Hazel) that she could not see Hazel's beauty. Emily knew Hazel was the most beautiful girl in Frosthold. When Emily was little, she loved her older sister. She followed her everywhere until her mother put a stop to that. But love turned into hatred when Emily grew a little older and started comparing herself to her older sister. Hazel's complexion, hair, and eyes made Emily insecure about herself. And their neighbors, friends, and kin didn't help either. Everyone talked about how beautiful Hazel was and how graceful she was. In truth, every lemon cake Emily ate was bittersweet. It was a testament to Hazel's superiority over Emily. But, of course, Emily was not aware of these thoughts. She just had a feeling inside her, a gnawing feeling that rose like a flame on sight or mention of Hazel. Now, this. Her Arthur. Emily had loved Arthur since she had first seen him. Being the son of a lieutenant, he was tall, dark, and handsome, just like heroes from the stories. She had told her mother and her friends, and she had made sure Hazel knew about him.

As much as Hazel liked the look on her sister's face, she did not like Arthur at all. He was a rich, haughty boy, who was the son of a rich, haughty man. She had seen how he talked with women and men who he deemed ugly and poor. He got into fights often. He was mean, and Hazel did not like mean people.

"I would rather marry Bubba, Father," said Hazel smiling as she looked at her sister and placed her hand on hers. "Emily likes Arthur. And Arthur and my temperament do not match. Maybe you should talk to him about Emily. She is—"

"You little rodent!" her stepmother snapped. "You dare show pity on my daughter." Anastasia spat, "This is what I think about your mother and you. All my life, I have suffered indignation because of her. I won't have my daughter go through the same thing. Save your pity for your dead mother, girl."

Tears streamed down Hazel's face. She got up, took her coat and scarf, pulled on her shoes, and ran outside the house. It was dark and cold, but she did not feel it. She ran through the yard and past the gate. Frostwing beat her wings and followed her. Into the forest, they went.

Hazel ran past tree after tree, clutching her scarf and tears streaming down her face. She ran half-blind. Her heart was beating furiously, protecting her from the cold. After a while, she grew tired and fell. She stood up. It was dark, and she could not see much. The sky was covered with treetops. She walked in the opposite direction, but it felt like she was going nowhere. She wandered around. Finally, she found a clearing with a tree in the middle. The sky was visible with the moon and the stars. She could see things under the moonlight, which made her less afraid. She decided to spend the night there until morning, or she may go farther and farther away. She sat down under the solitary tree in the clearing. Frostwing had followed her all the way, and now, the big bird sat in front of her, turning her head left and right. The realization struck

Hazel. She could ask Frostwing to show her the way.

"Frostwing! Can you help me return to my home?"

Frostwing hooted and nodded her head. Hazel felt elated. She beckoned Frostwing to come closer, and the owl obliged. The owl walked toward Hazel like a duck and jumped into her lap. "Oh, Frostwing, you sweet bird," said Hazel and massaged the owl's chin. The bird closed her eyes and purred in satisfaction.

A crackling sound caused Hazel to look up. And what she saw horrified her. At the edge of the clearing, perched on top of a tree was a pale, skinny little creature with two big round eyes. It was short with pale dry skin. It jumped down to the forest floor, and Hazel's heart jumped up inside her chest.

Frostwing flew away from Hazel and perched on the creature's shoulder. "Come back, Frostwing. He may hurt you."

Frostwing hooted and shrieked. "Do you know my bird, little girlie?" said the creature as he walked towards Hazel on all fours. "Yes, you do. You are the girl that feeds her. She has told me all about you."

An intense stench emanated from the crawling creature. Hazel wanted to run away, but she was frozen stiff from fear. "I will not hurt you," the creature said.

But Hazel did not believe him, and then, like a lightning, an animal came and stood next to her. A wolf. She screamed, but the wolf only nuzzled against her. She looked at the wolf's nose. It bore a scar. She had nursed him herself when he had come to her injured. The wolf at her side made her bolder. "Go away, or the wolf will hurt you. It protects me."

"Does it?" the creature said amused as he walked towards the wolf. He scratched the wolf's chin, and it whimpered like a puppy.

"You see, they love me too," said the creature and stretched his hands. Hazel saw animals lurking in the shadows, at the edge of the clearing. Hundreds of them. "Who are you?" she asked.

"I am King Frost."

"King Frost?" she gulped. "Will you kill me?"

"I am an old man driven out of my land. I protect these animals as you do. Besides, if I hurt you, they may tear me apart. That wolf seems particularly fond of you."

The wolf nuzzled at her fingers again. A fawn and a bear came over. She recognized them as well. With so many animals around, she felt more confident. When she looked back at King Frost, she saw a small creature in tattered clothing, shivering.

"I only ask for assistance, little girlie. With the Snow Queen sitting on the throne, it is freezing out here.

Could you give me that scarf?"

She slowly removed her scarf and handed it to him. The creature wrapped himself in it. "Ah, you are very kind indeed. Are you warm?" he asked Hazel.

"I am warm," she said smiling at him. She felt sorry for the poor thing. At least she had her coat.

"Could you give me your coat?" asked King Frost.

She hesitated but removed the coat and gave it to him. The icy wind made her shudder.

"Are you warm?" he asked again.

"Yes," she replied, making herself smile.

Then the creature's eyes grew wider, and his small mouth opened as if something just entered his mind. "Do you have a red stone on you?" he asked excitedly.

"Yes, I do. But how do you know?" she said.

"Give it to me."

"But it is a present—"

"For me," he said, ecstatic. "From my father. I know it. I don't know how, but I do."

When she handed him the stone, a bright light engulfed the creature. Hazel had to look away. When she looked back, she saw a regal figure standing in his stead. His crown, adorned with glittering jewels, sat atop his head. And his robes of rich velvet cascaded down his shoulders. King Frost looked like a real king.

"Are you King Frost?"

"Yes, Hazel, I am King Frost. Ages ago, I was the

ruler of this land. God punished me for being unkind to an old man. I was turned into the creature you saw earlier. God cursed me to roam this forest until someone kind came and saved me. Magic was also taken away from Frosthold. But now, it has returned because of your kindness."

"But ... I don't know what happened. It was the stone that did it."

"Your kindness reminded my father of the red stone that had once been part of my magical staff. It was a Christmas gift for me."

"Mr. Jerkins is your father."

"Yes, he is the old king. When magic was taken away, it was taken from everyone—me, my father, my son, and villagers too. The Snow Queen ruled the neighboring lands. She invaded Frosthold and turned every one of my men into an animal. She wiped their memories and everyone else's in Frosthold, so they forgot about old times."

Hazel looked at the animals around. Thousands of them had gathered. Birds, wolves, hounds, and bears.

"Hazel, how can I thank you?" said the king as he took her hands in his. "You must tell me a wish—any wish—and I shall grant it if it is within my power."

Hazel refused, but King Frost coaxed her. "You must tell me, Hazel."

"Can you ... can you bring my mother back to me?"

"That, I cannot do. Magic has certain boundaries. But, yes, I can bring her to this world for a few moments."

Hazel's eyes lit up with excitement. "Oh, I would love that, King Frost. Please, can you do that for me? I would be ever so grateful to you."

King Frost took a few steps back, murmured spells, and a womanly figure materialized under the moonlight. She was the most beautiful woman Hazel had ever seen. She shimmered under the moonlight, her figure levitating above the snowy ground. Her hair floated in the air. And her smile was the most magical. It was a warm, motherly smile. "Mother?" asked Hazel, with tears welling up in her eyes.

"Oh, Hazel," her mother said. "How I longed to talk to you. You are so beautiful, Child."

Hazel sobbed. She could not talk. Tears fell from her eyes and froze on the ground below. "Why did you leave me? Mother. Why?"

"I am so sorry, my dear child. I cried just like you in front of God and asked, why had he taken me away from my daughter?"

"Did you know how much I suffered?" Hazel asked, sobbing. Hazel never complained to her father, but she could not help herself in front of her mother. "They made me work all day, Mother. Nobody helped me. Even when I was sick, they made me work. They made me wear these clothes. Today, they left me alone at the house. They called me ugly and made me sleep in the kitchen. I never complained, Mother. I never complained. Even Father kept his silence."

"I know, Child," said her mother, tears flooding from her eyes, but the tears did not fall to the ground but vanished into thin air.

King Frost walked to the frail girl and hugged her. After she stopped sobbing, the king went down on his haunches and looked Hazel in the eyes. "You must be strong for your mother." The girl nodded her head.

"I am sorry, Hazel, for everything you suffered. You have lived a hard life. Harder than I ever knew possible. I know the things you went through. I feel bad for you, but I am happy. I am happy and proud because you are my daughter. Do you know who I feel sorry for? Your stepmother and your sister. You had a tough life, but you were stronger than your circumstances. They never broke you. They could not make you mean and cruel. The little your stepmother and your stepsister had to endure broke them. They suffer more than you know, Child. They suffer every day with pride, jealousy, and cruelty."

"Your stepmother, she hates you. I know that. She hates you because she lives in the shadow of a dead woman. You remind her of me. And Emily reminds her of her younger self. She worries about her daughter. She sees the same thing playing out between you two. And Emily, she is a nice girl, poisoned by her mother and jealous because she thinks you are better than her."

"Emily? She thinks I am better?"

"Yes, my sweet child. She has lived every moment of her life feeling inferior to you. And your father is a worried man. He worries Anastasia will leave him as I left him. Be kind to him, and go back."

"The time has come for magic and summer to return to this land," explained the levitating figure. "And you will be known as the Summer Queen."

"A queen ... me?"

"Yes, it is fate. Your stepmother, your sister, and all their friends will come and kneel before you, and they will love you."

Hazel did not know what to say to that. "Why me?" she asked.

"I don't know. But what I do know is if you had not been kind to Mr. Jerkins and King Frost, you would have wandered the forest and died frozen stiff. You were presented with choices, and you chose kindness. You saved yourself and saved King Frost from eternal damnation. He would have wandered this forest eternally. Your kindness has restored the magic within him and this land. He will rise again and reclaim his throne from the Snow Queen."

"I don't know what to say, Mother, except... except... that I love you. You are the loveliest of mothers. Your legacy guided me. I wanted to be like you. That was why I was kind. I had many unkind thoughts, but your memories—memories that I borrowed from Father, Mr. Jerkins, and your friends—guided me."

"I know, Child. I will always watch over you. I may not be with you in flesh and blood, but I will always be by your side. Remember that. I must take my leave now. It is time. I can feel it," said her mother and turned to King Frost. "I am grateful to you, Eddard. Please take care of my daughter." On hearing that, King Frost's cheeks flushed, and he said, "I must thank you and Hazel."

"Remember, Hazel. Be kind." At that, the smiling figure faded into darkness.

"Your mother is a lovely woman, Hazel. I am so glad to meet her," said King Frost. "I must do something if you can forgive me, Child." King Frost placed one hand on the ground, read some spells, and a transparent blue wave flew across the forest floor. Hazel felt a jolt when it reached her. The animals turned into men and women, wearing rich dresses and fine armor. The wolf, Hazel saw, turned into a young man with auburn hair and a mocking smile. He still had a scar on his nose. *The prince*, she thought. She saw Frostwing turn into a beautiful woman, which could have been no one else but the queen.

Each person inspected his clothes and body. They turned their hands and legs under the moonlight. They looked at each other and smiled. They laughed and cried. They hugged and shook each other's hands. They were happy to return.

"Silence!" the king's voice echoed through the forest. Everyone turned silent and stood straight. They were looking at Hazel. "Kneel," the king commanded and dropped down to one knee. The prince, the queen, and everyone else followed. Every man and woman. They knelt in front of the poor girl, wearing old tattered clothes.

The king stood and said, "My lady, we are grateful for your kindness. Now, you must do as your mother said. Go back to your father. We will return for you after everything is taken care of."

The king pointed at her, and her tattered clothing turned into a dress made of the finest silk, with a deep red hue that shimmered in the moonlight. "This was the Christmas present from your father. He planned to give it to you in secret. He will be surprised when he sees you in it."

The king pulled a ring from his hand and threw it on the snow. He waved his hands, and the ring turned into a gilt coach with two beautiful white horses. One of the soldiers jumped into the coachman's position. The prince opened the coach door and helped Hazel climb inside. They all waved and cheered as the horses began to walk.

Hazel sat inside the lavish coach, traveling to her home through the forest. She wondered what her father and stepmother would say. And Emily. She felt sorry for the poor girl. And then, Hazel saw a light stream into her coach. She had never seen morning light that bright. She looked out of the coach's window, and the snow shimmered under the sunlight. She looked above. The sun was so intense. It burned her eyes to look at it. *A change is coming*, Hazel thought. A change brought by kindness.

Epilogue: The Lesson Behind the Story

In the vast tapestry of life, the threads of kindness are the most beautiful and precious of all. A single act of kindness, no matter how small, can illuminate the darkest corners of the human heart and fill it with warmth and hope. It can inspire us to rise above our limitations, reach out to those in need, and sow the seeds of love and compassion in the world.

4

The Knotted Locks

Inspired by Rapunzel

When Noah's friend dies, he finds something unspeakable amongst his belongings. Something that could link him to the disappearance of a young girl. But when Noah sets out to uncover the truth about his friend, he'll get more answers than he bargained for.

Noah still couldn't believe Mr. Shingles was dead. He was his favorite customer. Maybe customer wasn't the right word. What would you call someone to whom you delivered free food thrice a week? Let's go with: Friend. Mr. Shingles was a friend. In the tiny coastal town of Rocky Surf, friends were few and far between. So, Noah took what he could get.

That being said, Noah liked to think he and Mr. Shingles would have become friends anyway, even if their circumstances had been different. Even with the chasm of a sixty-year age gap between them. Even with the controversy and disturbing rumors.

To all the Rocky Surf locals, Mr. Shingles was known as the Bird Guy. He wasn't built like a bird, though. In fact, he was quite a sturdy old fellow. If one were to assign animal attributes to Mr. Shingles, based on his physique, Walrus Guy would have been more accurate. Especially with that thick moustache that had covered everything from the bottom of his nose to the top of his chin. The good people of Rocky Surf often wondered how he had stayed so fat, since there was no visible way for food to get into his mouth.

He was called the Bird Guy because, well, birds just loved the old sod. Especially the seagulls. He would sit on his porch everyday from 4 am to 7 pm and just feed them.

"I'm going to tell Meals-On-Wheels to take you off

the list if you keep feeding all your food to the birds!" Noah used to tell him.

"Who's gonna feed them if I don't?" was Mr. Shingles's answer every time, and then he'd toss another handful of banana bread crumbs to his rowdy, winged audience.

But now, Mr. Shingles was gone, and all that was left of him was a cardboard box with Noah's name written on it. Noah sat on his bed with the mysterious box next to him. For some reason, he was scared to open it. It was probably just a few trinkets. Mr. Shingles had not had much, except for his birds. Noah dragged his hand through his black curly hair.

"What if it wasn't nothing?" he thought. What if it contained something he didn't want to see; something he didn't want to believe? What if it had something to do with that girl? The tall, blonde girl, who had gone missing ten years ago.

He gathered himself, held his breath, and opened the box.

Inside was something that looked like a photo album, and suddenly Noah was excited, he had never seen photos of Mr. Shingles before! He opened the album. He turned the first page, then the next, and then next. Faster and faster. There were no photos inside the album. Instead, what he saw sent a cold numbness rippling through his body.

Every page contained the same thing.
Locks, and locks of blonde hair.

Rapunzel – that's what the man called her – pulled on her hair. She had trouble remembering her real name. Everything before the room felt like fantasy or false memories. She wasn't sure about anything anymore. And now the man had taken away one of her only possessions a few days ago. A piece of sharp mirror she had used to cut her hair.

Out of sheer frustration, she brought the mirror to her hair and cut off most of it. What remained were irregular tufts of blonde on a bleeding scalp.

The door opened. It was the man. Who else? He had her daily tray of food with him, and he put it down on the cold, concrete floor. He said nothing and he looked furious. He had blindfolded himself, because he didn't want to see her like this. Rapunzel thought this was a bit over dramatic and childish for such a big old man. She didn't know why he was so obsessed with her hair. He would sometimes come in and sit behind her for hours, just running his fingers through her locks, murmuring in her ear. Sometimes the words were loving, almost as if he was comforting a daughter. Other times his breathing became ragged and his grip tightened on her head. Those times she could always feel something hard digging into the small of her back.

He slammed the door, putting the cherry on his tantrum.

"Ugh," she grunted, and looked at the tray of food at her feet. Same old, same old. Beans, boiled potatoes, shredded chicken and peas, and a piece of banana bread.

She broke off a piece of the bread, crumbled it into her pocket, and walked to her only window. It was high. She had to stand on her toes, and stretch her hand as far as she could, and then hold it there. Her stomach muscles burned. She kept her body in the awkward position until she could feel a light peck on her fingers.

She smiled. Her friend had come to visit again. He always did. She reversed slowly, surely, and Simon the seagull hopped, hopped into her room, ravenous for more treats.

Noah tried to think of a rational explanation for the locks of hair. He came up short. His mind was racing. His pulse banged in his temples like a kick-drum.

"Should I call the police?" he wondered out loud.

"What about the police, honey?" his mother yelled

from outside the door.

"Nothing Mom! Mind your own business!" he said with a quiver in his voice that he did not hide very well.

"You are my own business!" Her words bellowed through the keyhole. She laughed at her own joke and retreated down the stairs. Noah waited till he could not hear her footsteps anymore, and then returned his attention to the matter at hand.

He held one of the golden locks in his hand, and then foolishly thought, *my fingerprints*! But of course, his fingers couldn't leave prints on the hair. Then he thought about the album. Would it look suspicious if he wiped it clean? Noah was out of his depth.

He brought the hair to his nose. It smelled like apple shampoo. He immediately felt like a creep for doing that, but before he put it down, he noticed something intriguing about the lock of hair. At first he had thought the locks of hair were just tangled, but now he could see that there were little knots tied in it.

He opened the album again, and took out more strands of hair. He compared them to each other, and yes, they were all the same. They all had the same six knots.

Three knots, close together. And then three more, further apart.

Rapunzel held Simon the seagull tightly in her arms, but not too tight, so as not to hurt him. Other seagulls sometimes came to her room as well, but they never came inside. She could tell it was Simon and not one of the other gulls by his one glassy, blind eye.

Simon was getting old, though. He was flying into things, and his feathers had a withered look to them. This worried Rapunzel greatly. He was her only hope of getting out of this prison. If he died, she did not know how she would survive.

He made soft cawing noises. While she stroked his head, she took something out from under her worn out pillow. Simon knew what came next, and obediently lifted his leg. Even in her dire situation, Rapunzel could not get over how adorable it was.

She tied a lock of her knotted hair around his coarse leg, stood up and sent him on his way through her window.

Maybe this time, she thought.

Noah was sure that those knots were Morse code. What else could they mean? He was on his way now to Cruz, the old detective. He had fallen on hard times lately, and was also a Meals-On-Wheels customer like Mr. Shingles.

In the box on the back of his motorbike, Noah had Cruz's meals, the album of knotted locks, and a bottle of his dad's rum that he managed to sneak out of the house. He wanted to get Cruz's advice, and the only way to do that was to get the old man a little bit tipsy.

He had asked Noah for a bottle many times, but Noah had always refused. Today was different, though. He had to get some answers. He wanted to know for sure if his dear friend, Mr.Shingles, The Bird Guy, was some kind of pervert, or kidnapper, or murderer. Noah hoped beyond hope that he was wrong and that the collection of hair was just some weird hobby, like his birds had been.

He parked his bike outside the lighthouse where Cruz lived, and knocked on the heavy oak door.

"It's open!" said a gnarled voice.

"Hello, Detective Cruz, I've got a surprise for you." he said, holding the bottle of Kraken Black Spiced Rum in his arms like a new born baby,

The mountain of a man's eyes flickered like fireworks. "My boy," he said, "You shouldn't have!" But he had already taken two tumblers out of the cupboard. He gave Noah a massive bear hug to show his appreciation. He smelled weird to Noah. He had probably already started drinking today.

"I hope you don't mind drinking it neat. I don't have coke, or whatever you kids normally drink this with," he said, popping the cap.

"None for me, thanks. I'm sixteen, remember? I don't drink. But there is something you can help me with, Detective Cruz. Do you still have your Morse code chart?"

"Right there on the wall by the stairs," he said.

Noah put the two plates of food down on the table by which Cruz sat and plopped the album of hair down next to it. He decided he'll explain later. First, he wanted to find out what the code meant, if indeed it was a code.

When he got the chart on the wall, his eyes moved involuntarily up the stairs, and he could not help but notice the door at the top of it. It had three heavy locks.

Strange, he thought, and looked at the chart again. It did not take long to find what he was looking for. There it was, right at the top of the page. It was just as he had thought. Three dots and three dashes. The code was SOS.

He turned around hastily, and said: "Detective, I have something I want to show you."

The detective did not hear him. He was too busy turning the pages of the album. He looked red in the face. Noah couldn't figure out if he was mad, or just really, really drunk.

He inched his way toward the table. And as he got

closer, things started to connect in his brain. Like pieces of thread on one of those boards the FBI uses in television shows. Why did Cruz insist on always getting two plates of food? And why was the door at the top of the stairs locked like that?

"Come here, my boy," the ex-detective said in a gruff whisper. "Come sit here next to me."

Noah wanted to get the hell out of there, but instead, he tried to act cool and sat down next to Cruz, who put his hairy arm around him.

Then Noah recognized the smell wafting from Cruz. Rum, beer, and apple shampoo.

The kidnapper's stocky neck swivelled. They locked eyes. And they both grabbed at the half-empty bottle of rum.

A key turning in the door awoke Rapunzel. She shooed mosquitoes from her face, and then looked at the window to see if it was night or day. She decided it was some time in between.

The door at the top of the lighthouse groaned open, and without looking around she said, "What are you doing in here? I already ate. Did you bring back my mirror knife?"

"Ummm, no," the voice said. "Are you... are you...

Rebecca Shearer?"

"I don't know," she replied to the boy with the black bushy hair and a broken bottle in his hand.

"Rebecca Shearer, the girl who went missing."

"I'm not missing, silly, I'm right here. I've been right here. For a long time, too. He doesn't want me to leave. Are you friends with him?" The words rolled from her mouth in droves.

"C'mon, quick, let's get you out of here before he wakes up. I don't think... I don't think I killed him."

Simon flew into the room and landed on her scrawny shoulder, tap-tapping his feet to balance himself.

"I can't leave without Simon!" she said and hugged him to her chest with one arm. Simon pecked gently at her lips.

"That's fine!" said the boy. "Let's just go!"

He grabbed her by her free hand and led her out of her room. Was he a prince? Was she dreaming?

But as the boy placed his foot on the first step of the stairs and looked over his shoulder to ask if she was okay, there was a sound like rolling thunder coming toward them.

It was the bad man. He was hurt. She knew because his whole face was a red and sticky mess. His eyes glowered white through the mask of blood, and he stamped up the stairs.

"Look," she shouted.

By the time her prince finally turned his eyes back forward, the bad man was already halfway up the stairs.

"Leave Rebecca alone! She's mine," he screamed, and a mist of blood clouded the air in front of his face.

The boy hesitated for a moment, steadied himself, and leapt. Seems his plan was to tackle him, but the bad man lifted one fist in the air. Rugged knuckles dug deep into the boy's stomach, and he went sprawling over the railing. He hit the ground with a dull plop.

"Rebecca... Rapunzel... go back inside the room," the bad man said.

She weighed her options. She could go back into the room. But then she would stay forever, and the man would probably kill her prince. Or she could attack him! But if her prince couldn't manage to bring him down, how could she?

"Put that bird down! It's filthy," the bad man screamed, swaying on his feet. He was losing blood fast. Maybe she could take him after all.

She did as he said and put Simon down on the step-in front of her. With her other hand, she reached into her pocket and felt the rough texture of the banana bread crumbs.

"Okay," she said, and pretended to walk back to the room.

Just as the bad man let out a sigh, an exhale of relief,

she shot her arm out and opened her fingers. The crumbs darted toward his face, like a hundred tiny cannonballs, and stuck there in the congealing blood.

Simon went in for the kill.

The combination of surprise and loss of blood sent the bad man tumbling down the stairs, limbs flailing. When he hit the floor, Rebecca heard something snap. His arms and legs bent in impossible positions. Simon perched on his face and pecked at it voraciously.

"Are you okay?" she screamed at her prince as she descended the stairs.

"I broke my leg, I think," he answered.

"Yeah."

She helped him up. He put his arm around her neck, and together they half-hopped, half-walked. Warm light shone in through the front door.

"Are you a prince?" she asked, "Because I'm not a princess. I hope that's okay."

He laughed.

As they left the lighthouse, she gave one last glance at the bad man. Simon had finished all the crumbs, but he continued pecking in a mad frenzy. The poor thing was still hungry.

"Do you think he's still alive?" the boy asked.

"I hope so," she said.

Epilogue: The Lesson Behind the Story

This is a story with two morals. Firstly, always keep your eyes open. Things are rarely what they seem, especially people. Always be vigilant of your surroundings. You never know when someone who can't ask for it, might need your help. Secondly, always be kind to animals. They might just save your skin one day.

5

The Astounding Academy for Interesting Demons

Inspired by The Ugly Duckling

When you arrive at the bottom of the northern suburbs in the most unfathomable depths, go right at the river of peeled souls, turn left twice until you see a big mountain shaped like a goat's hoof and then go straight until you literally can't move anymore. Then, stop and turn around twice. It's across the road from McDonalds. You'll see it there, large as death. The Astounding Academy for Interesting Demons. You can't miss it.

Day 1

Inside the Astounding Academy for Interesting Demons, on a coffin-length bench studded with rusty nails, sat the smallest, plainest, most uninteresting demon in the underworld. The sad little thing's name was Poco.

Poco had no horns, no tentacles, no wings, no fangs, no powers, and no friends. You see, at the Astounding Academy for Interesting Demons, it was all about the glitz and the glam, and how many sets of teeth you had or how many types of venom you could squirt from your eyes. And poor Poco came up horribly short.

Poco had a hard time at school. He was bullied severely by a Minotaur named Greg. Greg would ask him things like, "Why are you so tiny and irksome?" And Poco, who knew for a fact that there was no right answer, which included shutting up, would say something like, "I'm Poco. I'm still growing!"

This confrontation would then be followed by either an acid bath, a stoning or a Big Bang Theory marathon. The last one was the worst. So many episodes.

Greg wasn't the only bully at the Astounding Academy for Interesting Demons. He had some nasty friends. Like Rich Clifford. He was half-pterodactyl, half-glow-worm, I think. And his other best buddy was Dementia, whose pronouns were your majesty, your highness, and Beelzebub. Poco was not exactly sure how to use those, but he tried his best. He always did.

He was Poco! Curse his little heart. He was still growing. And he was still learning.

Most of the demons that went to this school came from prominent demon families. Poco, on the other claw, had just kind of turned up one day. No one really knew where he was from, or who or what had spawned him. His appearance did not give away his bloodline either. He looked a bit like a spongy M&M. His features were unidentifiable. He looked like nothing, so that's how everyone saw him: Nothing.

The still-learning Poco was trying to figure out why this was so. Why was everyone like this to him? Why didn't he have any friends? What made him different? What would the other demons prefer him to look like?

Day 2

He sat at his marble desk at the back of Mrs. Lobe's Human Studies class. Mrs. Lobe looked like the lovechild of a rhinoceros and something else that might at one time have lived deep in the Mariana trench.

"OK, class, quiet down please," said Mrs. Lobe. "I have

a surprise for you."

"What is it?" shouted Gnarles, a gila-monster-ish boy with debilitating halitosis.

Mrs. Lobe threw a large potted ficus at him and missed on purpose. "Keep your little hellholes shut and I'll tell you, Gnarles." Everyone went dead quiet. Everyone except for the cricket-girl at the back, who really couldn't help it. Mrs. Lobe lifted a cardboard box onto her table.

"I went to the human world and robbed a library! Yay!"

This was not what they expected, and even the cricket-girl was quiet now.

"Mr. Darth showed us a human sacrifice video on HellTube," Gnarles whispered, his tail covering his mouth.

"I said, "I went to the human world, and robbed a library!" Mrs. Lobe repeated, much louder, and picked up another, larger potted plant.

"Yaaaaay!" everyone exclaimed.

She handed out the 'borrowed' books, and everyone received one. Gnarles got a Zulu version of *Harry Potter and the Prisoner of Azkaban*. "Ah, no, I've already read this one, Miss!" he said.

Cricket-girl got *Dante's Inferno,* and she said, "This is cultural appropriation, Miss."

A wraith in a human-skin fedora got *Fifty shades of*

Grey and whispered an incantation.

And Poco received a square book, with lots of pictures and thick pages. He read the title: *The Ugly Duckling*.

"Wanna swap?" Poco asked the wraith, who hissed violently and clutched the book tight to where its chest was supposed to be. "I guess not."

That night Poco went home – the janitor's closet – and read *The Ugly Duckling* over and over, until the thick baby-friendly pages started coming loose. Suddenly he understood. Small explosions were happening inside his brain. His instincts kicked in and he knew what he had to do.

Poco was learning.

Day 3

The following day, Poco strutted into the Astonishing Academy for Interesting Demons with sparkly new confidence. Everyone pointed at him and gasped, and Poco braced himself for Oooh's and Aaah's. He promised himself he would not get a big head. He'd still be the same old Poco when he had popularity and friends, and... white feathers all over.

"Is that a chicken?" someone shouted, and the whole hallway burst out laughing.

Tears streamed from Poco's eyes, and he retreated

hastily to his closet and was irritated to find the janitor there.

"What's wrong, little one?" asked the janitor, who was human, by the way.

"Nothing," snorted Poco, ruffling his feathers.

"Are you hungry? Is that what's wrong?"

"No... Why?"

"Oh, it's just, I saw you ate that book yesterday. I can give you cheeseburger?"

Poco declined the burger, but asked the janitor if he could perhaps borrow his pretty sweater. He then pulled the sweater over his head and roamed through the halls of the school, like a checkered ghost. No one noticed him. He observed. He listened. He learned.

Day 4

Poco saw many things as he lurked around the school. For instance, he saw a group of girls admiring Greg the Minotaur's horns and the large golden ring in his nose.

Day 5

Poco felt like himself again. A new, better self, with majestic curling horns and a shiny ring through his nose. He tried to pluck his white feathers, but they grew back overnight.

"You look amazing! What's your name?" a girl demon with nine tails asked him, and blew him a kiss.

"I'm Poco, I'm still growing," said Poco, and more girls started hanging around him.

"Poco, are you new?"

They scratched his belly and polished his horns, and made him feel special. He even let some of them try on his nose ring. Suddenly, Poco's life had become amazing. More and more, girls and guys started hanging around him. Everyone loved him, except a few of them, Poco noticed. A small pack of demons still followed Rich Clifford around.

They admired his long beak and veiny wings, and they complimented his squishy body and ability to glow in the dark. And for the first time in his life, little Poco, who was still growing and still learning, felt the black tendrils of jealousy penetrate him.

No one noticed this. No one noticed Poco's eyes turning dark. No one noticed his smile turning into a scowl. No one noticed the posters on the lockers that said:

"MISSING DEMON. HAVE YOU SEEN GARY THE MINOTAUR?"

Day 6

The next day, there were more posters. This was also the day Poco came to school with another new, fresh look. This time, little Poco had white feathers, bull horns, a ring through his nose, a long beak, large bat-like wings, and the ability to glow in the dark.

More demons noticed him. More demons hung around him, and Poco noticed more demons that did not notice him. Dementia, who had lost two of her friends, watched from a distance.

Day 7 - 14

More posters appeared, and Poco grew more unique each day. Now he also sported scales, clawed feet, a trunk on his back, and eyes on the tips of his fingers.

He was gorgeous.

Other demons no longer huddled around him, they started following him in a procession. They screamed his name, played hellish instruments, and implanted themselves with a myriad of extensions. They just wanted to be like Poco.

Day 15

Something bad happened. There were more posters up in the Astounding Academy for Interesting Demons, but they weren't for missing demons. All the posters said:

"LESS IS MORE".

Signed, D.

Now still growing, still learning Little Poco felt another new emotion, and it shot through his body like an acid spewing volcano. His whole body got hot. From the tips of his horns to the end of the trunk on his back, anger consumed Little Poco.

He flew around the school like a rabid Tasmanian devil, and ripped off all the posters. His fan club watched his rampage closely and decided this was not a good look for him.

First, ten stopped following him, then twenty, then fifty. Eventually, only a few die-hard demons remained.

That night, he went home to his closet, found a jigsaw and sawed off all his new appendages. But alas, everything just grew back. He had to make another plan. And he did.

Day 16

Little Poco could hardly fit through the school's doors anymore, but he squeezed through and he found Dementia.

He looked at her with flaming eyes.

She started to say something.

"I know what you—"

Before she could finish, he ate her, right then and there with one loud gulp, in front of all the other students. One would think that an event like this wouldn't matter much to demons. I mean, they study subjects like medieval torture, blood rituals, and the summoning of the Dark Lord. But apparently, this was too much, even for them.

They screamed and sprinted around the halls like headless chickens. But Little Poco, who now had Dementia's long, stretchy tentacles, grabbed them one by one and stuck them into his mouth. Some of them, he swallowed whole. The ones he liked less, he chewed a few times.

He gobbled up everyone. The cheerleaders, the jocks, the nerds, the faculty. Even the poor janitor. No one was left undigested.

He ate, swallowed, absorbed, and devoured until he was the only demon left. By now, he was so big and so disfigured that he had broken through the roof of the

Astounding Academy for Interesting Demons. More of him was now outside the destroyed school than inside.

Next to the school ran the river of Hades, and Poco saw himself reflected in it. He saw what he had become, and he was horrified.

He growled in a voice that shook the unfathomable depths. "AM I BEAUTIFUL?"

And no one answered. Because there was no one left.

"I'm sorry," he said into the nothingness. "I'm Poco, I'm still growing."

Epilogue: The Lesson Behind the Story

Finding your identity can be difficult, but in the end, you can't expect others to love you if you don't first love yourself. Remember to embrace who you are, even if you don't know who that is yet. If you stay true to yourself, you will blossom into something amazing. If you keep changing to please everyone around you, you will end up pleasing no one. Least of all, yourself.

6

Dad's Wrestling Match

Inspired by Little Red Riding Hood

Rachael, a teenager, grapples with the conflicting impulses of youth and adulthood. When a charismatic and mysterious man named Joe Mama appears at her doorstep, Rachael's world is turned upside down. As the story unfolds, we are drawn into a dark and foreboding world of violence, power, and manipulation.

Rachael came down from her room into the kitchen. Her father was sitting and reading the newspaper. Her mother was preparing breakfast.

What is he reading the newspaper for? thought Rachael. *On Saturday, you should go out and have fun.*

Rachael knocked on the table. "Dad?"

Gary lowered his newspaper. "What?"

"Would you take me to the bowling alley tonight? I am going out with Emily and her boyfriend."

"Only if you promise you will go to Grandma's tomorrow."

She hesitated and then said. "I promise."

Gary eyed her. "I don't believe you, but let's see."

Rachael heard her mother speak. "Why don't you come with me and Sam tonight, Rachael? We will go shopping, and I will treat you to a nice dinner. You do not want to be a third wheel, hanging around those two."

Rachael's ears turned hot. "The only reason I don't have a boyfriend is because of you two."

Her mother laid out two plates on the table. "You do not have a boyfriend because you are thirteen."

"Whatever. I don't even care. Boys my age are not even interesting."

"When do I pick you up?" asked her father as he folded up his newspaper.

"I will call you."

"What do you mean you will call me? Tell me now, or you are not going. There are a lot of shady men around there."

"Men don't scare me."

"Then you are stupid," said her father as he picked up the sandwich. "They scare me."

Rachael was skeptical. She had seen her father get into fights all the time. One time, they were at Sam's wrestling tournament, and Gary got into a scuffle with someone else's father who was heckling Sam.

"I will kick them in the balls if anyone ever tries anything with me," said Rachael with food in her mouth.

"Rachael!" said her mother, turning to look at Rachael. "Mind your language."

"You think it is that easy?" said Gary as he wiped his mouth on a napkin. "Sam!" he called out. "Sam!"

The scrawny ten-year-old Sam came into the kitchen wearing only his shorts. Gary stood up. "Stand up, Rachael. Let's see how you do."

Gary walked out of the house into his front yard. The kids followed. The grass was freshly cut, and the ground felt soft beneath their naked feet. Both kids stood, facing each other, with Rachael a head taller than her brother. Sam had red hair and freckles on his face. His hands were like twigs. Rachael smiled knowingly.

"On the count of three, you will try to kick him between the legs, and he will try to pin you down," said Gary with an amused look.

"One. Two. Three! Go!"

Rachael kicked. Sam caught her legs with his left hand and then shot a takedown. Rachael was down on the ground with her brother on top. She tried to move her hips to get up but could not break free from Sam's hold. Sam was laughing as she tried to scratch his face. He simply grabbed her wrist.

"Sam, get up," she said, but he was not listening.

She pulled her right hand from Sam's grip and slapped him across his face. That seemed to do the trick. Sam loosened up. Rachael pulled her hips from under him and kicked him in the chest. Sam fell on his butt on the grass. She stood up. Sam was crying.

"Why did you hit him?" asked Gary as he pulled Sam to his feet.

"That was a street fight. Not a wrestling match."

"Rachael," a voice called out from across the street. It was David. He was a nerd. Every time Rachael saw him, he reminded her of a mouse with his squeaky voice and small face. She was a little taller than him. Her mother told her that boys grow late. Rachael believed her, but she did not believe David would outgrow her because she could not see it in her mind. Rachael thought anything she could not imagine was unlikely. For instance, she struggled to imagine someone overpowering her. Many of her friends feared walking in dark alleys or alone at night. Rachael feared the dark, but she thought nothing of men. Like David, most of them were stuttering idiots.

David was crossing the street with a stupid smile and a book in his hands.

"Hey, David. Look out," said her father as David almost got hit by a car.

He walked up to them, smiling nervously. "Hi, Gary. Hello, Rachael. Hi, Sam. I saw you guys wrestling from across the street. Having fun uh?"

Rachael snatched the book from his hand. "What do you have here, David?"

"Hey, that's not nice, Rachael," said her dad. Sam was wiping his tears.

"It is fine, sir. She is my friend," said David, smiling.

Rachael looked at him and forced a smile. "Yes, we are." She looked down at the book in her hand. It had a blue cover with golden inscriptions of fairies, castles, and dragons, and "Grimm's Fairy Tales" was written in the middle.

"That's a good book, David," said Gary, with his hands on his hips. "I used to read Rachael and Sam one tale each day. Rachael used to like the tale of Little Red

Riding Hood."

"I would have never thought Rachael would enjoy fairy tales."

"Why not! She used to love 'em. I had to buy her a red cloak. She would go around on Halloween with a little basket in her hand like the girl in the tale and ask for treats."

"Isn't that the one where the little girl strays from a path, which leads to her getting eaten by the wolf?"

"And the grandma," said Gary. "It is one of the few dark fairy tales. I think that is why Rachael loved it because it was so different from the others."

"It is a sexist story," said Rachael, handing David the book back. "It is an attempt to subjugate young girls. You will get eaten if you do not stay on the right path."

"Maybe," said David, "but isn't it true? For everyone? If you do not do the right thing, you could get into trouble."

"And what is the right thing?"

"Listening to your parents," said Gary as he patted David on the back. "So, David, what brings you here?"

"I just came here to tell Rachael I have completed the group project."

"A group project?" said Gary, lifting his eyebrows at Rachael. "I hope you had a group with you."

Rachael eyed David. "Of course, Rachael and I brainstormed together on the phone. She provided most of the ideas."

"Oh yes, she is really good at telling people what to do. Too bad she is not good at listening," said Gary.

Looking at Rachael's father, David forced himself a smile and then looked at Rachael, gazing downward and tapping the raw ground with the front of her feet. David wondered if Rachael was embarrassed.

Gary dropped Rachael at the bowling alley. He would pick her up at 10 p.m. Emily was already there with her boyfriend Mark, who was as plain as her. They were both sixteen years old and did as they were told. Mark had sandy-colored hair and precisely three acne spots on his chin. They were probably the only interesting thing about him in Rachael's eyes.

Both wore T-shirts and shorts. Rachael herself was wearing a white dress and a denim jacket. She was worried she had overdressed until she saw her date, Henry, arrive. He was wearing a pink suit. Rachael thought the pink matched well with her denim and white dress, but she did not want to be a subject of derision in the school by dating a pink boy. Thankfully, she was with Emily, who did not gossip and was very accepting. Girls her age in her school were jealous of her because all the boys buzzed around her, and she did not like to admit it, but she led them on.

"Oh, hi, guys. How long have you been standing here?" asked Henry. "You arrived early uh?" Henry was tall and handsome, but his voice still had not matured. When he talked, he reminded her of Sam.

The group walked past the bowling alley and into the restaurant next to it. They did not want to run into kids from their school. A lot of young people frequented the bowling alley. Rachael did not understand why. The boys always tried to impress girls there, but she doubted any girl would be impressed by a guy knocking down a bunch of bowling pins. At least the guys were graceful. Girls almost always embarrassed themselves. She did not want anyone, especially herself, to feel insecure about their incompetence in an irrelevant game that nobody enjoys, at least not for a long time, so she had advised them to go to the restaurant next to the bowling alley.

The restaurant was dimly lit. Most of the customers were adults. It was a semi-fancy restaurant. Rachael had stolen $100 from her father's wallet in case Henry did not bring the money. As it happened, she was wise to do so. Henry refused to order anything for himself except for a milkshake. Only when Rachael implied that she paid her tabs on dates that Henry ordered himself sushi.

Rachael ate only sparingly. She had been excited to go on a date. She never imagined it would be this awkward: attempting to start a conversation, feigning interest, and pretending to be nice. Adults had an easier time finding common interests. They could bond over the movies they have watched, and the hobbies they have, and they could talk about religion. If everything fails, they always have politics to discuss. If you have lived long enough, you will have something in common with the other person—something you can share. But when you are a thirteen-year-old girl with an expectation that comes from movies, it is difficult not to feel disappointed. Rachael shifted uncomfortably in her seat, playing with the straw in her drink as she scanned the room for any sign of excitement.

Emily and Mark were absolutely into each other. They talked with smiles on their faces. Emily felt sick of the music playing in the background. *I should have gone shopping with Mom and Sam*, thought Rachael. She realized she was not even interested in Henry. She agreed to the date because she had heard Sophia brag about going on dates. When you were thirteen, even meager things such as driving, drinking, and makeup gave you bragging rights. Rachael had tried each one of them. She drove and slammed her mom's car into a garbage bin. She drank at a sleepover and was subsequently banned from attending any in the future. And when she wore makeup at school, her mother was called to the principal's office.

The restaurant was almost empty. The server was looking at them as if she wanted them out, probably understanding she would not get tips. She watched the dust swirl under the streetlight as she nodded her head. Rachael was getting tired of Henry talking about Final Fantasy and trying to convince her to watch anime. She was more of a K-culture fan. And everybody knew Japan and Korea did not get along. Rachael was on Team Korea.

"We should go. My dad is coming to pick me up in fifteen minutes," said Rachael and paid half of the bill.

She welcomed the fresh air outside. Henry came and stood next to her. "You don't have to wait."

"No, it is fine," said Henry. Rachael clenched her teeth.

Emily and Mark came outside, laughing and touching each other. "You should have told me when you came outside Rachael," said Emily, looking at Rachael and realizing what was happening.

Emily whispered something to her boyfriend who said to Henry. "I think we should head out, man."

"I just want to accompany her till her father comes to pick her up. I can't leave her alone at night."

"Emily will be with her," said Mark, taking Henry by the elbow. "Her father would not be thrilled to see her with you."

Rachael and Emily were alone when a red convertible drove by in the street. It slowed down where they were standing. And sitting in the driver's seat was a boy wearing a white T-shirt, a red bandana on his forehead, and a sly smile. He looked like the sidekick from the '80s Karate Kid. The boy that shouted, "Put him in a body bag." Her father had made sure she and Sam had watched that movie. Rachael was not very enthusiastic about it, but she secretly loved it.

The boy in the red car was driving back toward them, but her father pulled up in front of them. Rachael got in and invited Emily inside. They waited until Rachael's mother came to pick her up.

Rachael saw the red car still standing as she drove back to her home.

Rachael crossed her arms and huffed. "I really don't want to go to Nana's today, Dad."

"But you promised," he said sternly.

"I know, but I just don't feel like it. Can't I stay home?"

"You know we always go to Nana's on Sundays after

church," her dad said.

"But Dad, can't I just skip it this time? I promise I'll be safe at home," Rachael pleaded.

Her dad exhaled deeply, clearly frustrated. "Fine, whatever. Do what you want but you know the rules, keep the doors locked."

Rachael's face lit up with relief, "Thank you, Dad. I will."

Rachael sat in the front yard as her family went into the car. Sam and her mother were in the back. Her dad was in the front, wearing a polo shirt. *Who wears a polo shirt to church?* She had a glass of orange juice in her hand and a summer dress on her. She felt happy this morning.

"Go inside, Rachael," shouted her father from inside the car.

"Have fun, Dad." She had a smile on her face. She knew what her grandmother's house would look like. There will be little kids shouting, crying, and running around. The dads would barbecue with flies buzzing around from her garden. Her cousin Olivia would be there. Everyone will talk approvingly of her. She was a good Christian girl who did what she was told. She is good in school, and she listens to her parents. She did not go on dates or lie. When Rachael would be mentioned, her mother would have a disapproving expression on her face although she would rather have Rachael as her daughter instead of Olivia because Rachael was more beautiful.

It was getting hotter by the minute, so Rachael went inside and turned on the TV but did not lock the door.

———◈———

Rachael heard the sound of an engine roaring. The car was too loud to be on the street. She got up, straightened her dress, and walked to the main door. Looking through the screen door, she saw a red convertible parked in her driveway. *The car from last night.* The dents and scratches were covered with car stickers, which made the car look worse. In daylight, the car looked run down when it had looked fresh under the streetlight.

The driver was the same boy she had seen last night. He wore a red bandana that covered his sandy-colored hair and thick black sunglasses that made him look silly. Rachael noticed he also had a friend with him this time. His friend was bald and wore a puffed-up jacket as if it were winter.

The boy saw her looking at him. "Hey, what's up?"

"Who are you?" she asked from behind the screen door. She knew damn well who he was but did not want to tell him she had noticed him.

"We met last night," he said, with one hand on the steering wheel.

"We did not. I do not know who you are," she said, with the TV show playing in the background. "If I had seen you, I would remember. You look silly."

"I am Joe. Joe Mama. Let's go for a ride," he said, with a sly smile on his face. "I bet you have not been on a ride with a boy yet."

"I've gone on plenty of rides," Rachael lied from behind the screen. She knew she should walk away from the door but did not.

He opened the car's door and climbed out but stumbled. Rachael giggled. He straightened himself.

"Who is your friend?" she asked. The friend had not looked towards her once. His face stared straight ahead, but Rachael felt his eyes dart behind those thick black sunglasses.

"That's my friend Aljamain. He is really quiet. He can sit in the back, and we can sit in the front. It will be really nice. We can go to the beach."

The beach was a two-hour drive away. She could never visit there without her family coming back. They might still be in church, though, for all she knew. She started to calculate but gave up and decided to feign uninterest. "I don't know who you are."

"Come on, Rachael, I live just around here," said Joe

Mama.

"I have never seen you around. Wait, how do you know my name?"

"I know everybody's name around here. I know what they do. I know where they live. I know where your family is. They have gone to your grandma's right now. I know how long they won't be here," said Joe Mama, strolling towards the screen door as if he was climbing a hill.

Feeling squeamish in her stomach, Rachael locked the door.

"What's the lock going to do?" asked Joe Mama in a meandering tone. "It is just a screen door. That friend of mine out there," he said, pointing towards Aljamain. "He can break that door down like it was made of cardboard."

"You are scaring me," she said, pulling at the door. Her hand felt clammy on the door handle.

"There is no need to be scared. We are friends. I just want you to go on a ride with me. That's all. Aljamain will sit in the back," said Joe Mama as if he was rhyming. "We will sit in the front."

"My mother will be angry at me."

"Your mother is jealous, Rachael. She was never as beautiful as you. Your folks are jealous. They don't know it, but they are. They don't want you to have fun."

Joe Mama reached the staircase in front of the screen door. Aljamain had gotten out of the car and was leaning against it, looking around.

"Can I go inside and change my clothes?" asked Rachael. Her phone was on the couch. She would call her father or the police. She could not decide. Rachael gulped.

"There is no need for that, Rachael. You look great in that dress. Just open the door and come out like that," said Joe Mama as he reached the screen door.

She turned a little to walk inside. "Just wait ..."

"Do not go inside! What did I tell you, Rachael? Whatever you do. Do not go inside. I will break that door. You think this door will keep me away from you? I will tear it down, and when your family comes back, I will tear them down. You understand. If you come quietly, nobody gets hurt."

Rachael was shaking. She knew she should block the door with the chair and run inside and get her phone, but she could not move. Suddenly, she saw the boy's face. It was not a boy's but a man's. He had leathery skin, and she could see a receding hairline behind the red bandana. *Am I going to die today?* she thought, her mind swirling with confusion.

"How old are you?" she asked. "You look like you are in your thirties."

His face flared at that. "I am only nineteen. Everyone

knows it. And Aljamain is twenty-one."

He might have been only an inch taller than Rachael. His limbs were skinny, but he had a round gut on him.

"What are you watching?" he asked, changing the subject. "Modern Family? Maybe we could go to the movies. What do you say?" His voice was sweet as if he had not threatened her just a minute ago.

Rachael felt regret for not listening to her father. She should have gone to church. She should have listened to her parents. She had strayed from the path, and the big bad wolf had come to eat her.

"Why are you doing this? I am scared. Please go," said Rachael.

"Look," he said, pausing and supporting himself with his left hand on the wall. "You do not want us to bust through that door," he said, forcing a smile on his face. "You do not want us to hurt your brother, Sam, your sweet mother, or your father. So, come out like a sweet little girl."

"You can't hurt my father. He was a wrestler," said Rachael, feeling stupid for saying it.

Both men laughed. Aljamain had almost reached the staircase and was walking towards the door.

The man fished in his back pocket and pulled out a pocket knife. "Wrestlers bleed all the same," he said, and his expression darkened. "I am getting tired of your bullshit. You come out here and go sit in that vehicle quietly. Or else ...," he said, banging his hand on the screen door. "I am going to bust through this door."

Rachael backed away, startled. She shook her head. The door handle rattled as Joe Mama tried to open the door.

"Please stop. I am coming. Please," said Rachael. The rattling of the door was more horrifying than the men standing behind it. She did not want them to get angry. She felt they would be worse if they had to break the door. Rachael walked towards the door slowly. Joe Mama took a back step and put the knife inside his pocket, raising his hand and eyebrows.

The door opened with a click. "That's right," said Joe Mama, licking his lips. Rachael dragged the door open.

"You go start the car, Aljamain. Let me bring the lady over."

She walked out with her head down. He put a hand over her shoulder. She squirmed inside his grip.

Rachael heard the car starting as she walked into the harsh sun. She felt cold. Her head swirled. She felt as if she was going to faint.

Gary saw his daughter being led to a red convertible parked outside his house. He had been mad at her as he sat in the church. He had felt uneasy, so he had decided to drive back to his house and take Rachael to his mother's with her. Church was only two miles away. His wife and Sam were sitting outside waiting for him to bring Rachael back with him.

Rachael did not look right. She was moving slowly. Her posture drooped. When he saw her almost faint, Gary knew something was wrong. He pushed the gas. The bald man sitting in the car saw Gary's car through the rearview, and he sped away, leaving his friend behind.

Gary stopped the car in the same spot the red car had been and got out. The other guy looked startled. He was looking at Gary and the red convertible that had sped away. When Gary stood before him, he said, raising his hands. "Hey, man, we were just going to the beach. She invited me last night. I was here to pick her up."

Rachael ran to her dad, crying.

"Rachael, go sit in the car," her dad yelled, his eyes on the man. She did. "Who the fuck are you, you midget? How old are you? Forty years old?" he asked.

"Let me go, man," said the man, his eyes darting sideways.

"Don't you fucking move," shouted Gary, as his face turned red, veins popping out of his neck.

Rachael sat in the car, looking out. She saw fear on the man's face. But her fear for herself had turned to her father. *Just let him go, Dad,* she thought. And then Joe Mama ran. Her father followed. As he ran, Joe Mama pulled out his knife, and he stopped when he realized he could not outrun her dad. He pulled out a knife and turned to face her father. Gary stopped. Rachael got out of the car and ran toward them. Joe Mama was slicing the air as her father tried to reach him. Her father feinted, ducked under the knife slicing through the air, and tackled Joe Mama. A terrible scream rose in their peaceful neighborhood. She saw many men running towards the scene. Her neighbors had come out.

    Rachael could not see what had happened. She saw only the back of her father and the legs of Joe Mama underneath him. She moved to the right to see at an angle and saw blood. Her stomach tightened. Gary was pushing the knife into the man's shoulder, trying to keep Joe Mama down. His bandana had flown away, and his sunglasses lay on his side smashed. Gary said, looking up at the men that were gathering around, "Someone, please call the police." As other men held Joe Mama down, her dad got up and came to her. He had blood splattered all over his hand and face. He hugged her. Rachael cried in his arms, not caring about getting blood all over her dress. She had met the wolf. She promised herself she would keep true to the right path. *What was the right path?* She knew the answer. She had always known the answer. It was her conscience. Almost always, she knew the right thing to do. And in case her conscience was wrong, well, she tried. There is nothing more she could do except what she knew to be right.

Epilogue: The Lesson Behind the Story

No matter our gender, we must always be mindful of the predators that may be lurking in unexpected places. And while the story is targeted towards young women, men are not exempt from the dangers of life. By being aware and informed, we can better protect ourselves and those around us. Remember, it's not about living in fear, but rather being prepared and empowered to handle any situation that may arise.

And, guys, let's not be the wolves in the story, but rather the knights in shining armor. Treat women with the dignity and respect they deserve, because let's be honest, it's not that hard. All it takes is being a decent human being and treating others the way you want to be treated.

7

The Seven Bros

Inspired by Snow White

---◈---

*E**verything can change in the blink of an eye. When a normal college guy visits his crush's dormitory, a drastic change in the demeanour of the resident bros causes panic and pandemonium. Can he get himself and his crush to safety before they become lunch, or worse?*

Silas glided the mouse pointer over the laptop screen. There was a click, and then a song by Machine Gun Kelly blasted through the tiny speakers.

"Woah," I said.

"Sorry," said Silas, and he turned the volume down just a bit. "Just watch."

The video transitioned through short clips of young guys running around, knocking back beers, playing video games. Caught in the act of a range of energetic shenanigans.

The music stopped abruptly, and a guy with a smile the size of a slice of watermelon jumped in front of the camera.

"Welcome to the house of bros!" said the ecstatic guy on the video. "Let me show you around the place!"

"Who's that happy guy?' I asked.

"That's Pills," said Silas.

"Pills?"

"Yeah, we all got nicknames when we moved into the dorm. His name's Pills, because no one can be *that* happy. He has to be on something."

I snickered.

"What's your nick—"

"Shut your mouth and watch the video," said Silas, and he placed his hand on mine. I looked down at our touching fingers and tried to hide my smile by furrowing my brow.

"So, the other seven bros and I were quite lucky to get this amazing old-ass building to live in. No one wanted it because it's 'falling apart' and 'we're going to die,'" Pills continued, using air quotations. "But we ain't afraid of nothing!"

I looked around Silas's room and noticed the paint coming off the walls like dandruff, and missing planks in the hardwood floor, but he took my skull in his hand and rotated it until I faced the laptop again.

"We all actually have our own floor. Isn't that sick? But I'm just gonna take you to the party area where us bros go to kick back," Pill continued, and then suddenly the camera pointed at a bunch of guys lounging on two raggedy couches, sharing a bucket of chicken nuggets. "Let me introduce you to the bros!"

The camera moved from bro to bro, and Pills introduced each of them.

"This here is Cyrus the Virus, because he's always sniffling and sneezing."

"Hi," said a red-nosed Cyrus, crumpled tissue in hand.

"This big, grumpy dude over here is Hulkules. You can probably guess why we call him that."

A guy with a tiny head and arms as thick as railroad ties grunted at the camera.

"Over here we got our resident geek, The Prof."

"I prefer Resident Nerd. And I'm the only one in this

whole eight story death trap that's going to pass this semester," said The Prof, adjusting his glasses.

"That guy holding the bucket of chicken like he's scared it's gonna fly away is Shaggy."

"Hi," said Shaggy, and he gave a small wave a few seconds too late. Spicy oil dripped from his fingers.

"That guy without the face is Hoodie."

A guy with his face tucked deep inside the shadows of a black hoodie raised his arm and then his middle finger.

"Don't mind him, he's just shy," said Pills. "And this last guy is Catnap."

The camera points to a guy lying facedown on a not-so-clean floor. Pills gave him a little kick, and Catnap did not even stir.

"What about Snow White?" asked a voice off camera, followed by a sneeze.

"Yeah!" grunted another.

"Oh, I almost forgot," said Pills, and then he grabbed the camera and turned it around.

"The last bro is...drumroll... Snow White!"

"Okay, okay, hi everyone," said the Silas on the laptop screen

"I still need to edit that out," said Silas on the chair next to me, and he paused the video.

"Snow White?" I asked.

"Yeah, it has to do with me feeding birds in the park

on my own. A few pigeons came and sat on my head and shoulders, and I sang to them. Like in that movie."

I was slightly taken aback by his nickname, and it showed on my face.

"Yeah, I know, I know. It's embarrassing," said Silas.

"No, it's not that. Don't you find it a bit... racist?" I asked carefully.

"What? Because I'm from Kenya? No way. It's just a joke between us bros. And it makes for a good ice breaker at parties."

"Ok, then," I said, even though I did not like it.

I really liked Silas. Like, really, really liked him, and I didn't want a bunch of idiots making fun of him and the color of his skin.

"By the way, I didn't even get a piece of that apple pie you sent. They guys, the bros I mean, ate all of it."

"That's okay," I said with a forced smile. I couldn't believe those imbeciles had eaten the pie. I baked it for Silas and Silas alone, with love. I wonder which one of the doofuses from the video had gotten the slice with pastry heart.

My blood boiled.

"Hey, I'm sorry," said Silas, and gave my hand a hard squeeze. "If it's any consolation, I saw on social media that there is some kind of virus going around in apples. How weird is that?"

"Yes, weird..." I whispered, having no clue what he

had just said. I was so enraptured in his eyes and his lips. I couldn't wait any longer. I moved in for a kiss.

But all of a sudden, something loud crashed through the door. The frame spat splinters and larger fragments of wood in all directions. On the floor, amidst the debris of the door, lay a person.

"Holy shit! Who is that?" I yelled, but as he came to his feet, I recognized him from the video.

"Hoodie, are you okay? What the hell just happened?" asked Silas.

His face was deep inside his hood, and his head hung forward. With every step he took toward us, a dollop of thick red liquid spewed from where I supposed his mouth was and splattered to the floor.

"Shit, he's hurt," I said. "I'll call the hospital." I took out my phone and started tapping away, but before I could press send, Silas tugged at my sleeve.

"Look…" he whispered.

Hoodie's hood had fallen from his head, and now his face was revealed in all its gruesome glory.

Where Hoodie's left eye had been, there was now only a wet hole, while his right eye darted in all directions. Only half of his nose was left, and it leaked blood in a regular flow. He had the look of a ravaged rat after a stray cat had taken a few bites of it and decided to move on to its next prey. Where Hoodies' skin wasn't matted with red, it was a waxen gray.

As he growled, red foam bubbled from his lips.

"I'm calling the hospital, Hoodie! You're going to be alright," I yelled.

But Hoodie did not show any sign of having heard what I had said. Instead, he leaped at Silas and pinned him to the floor.

Silas screamed, "Hoodie! It's me! It's your bro, Silas!"

Hoodie gave zero F's.

Hoodie's head was in line with Silas's chest, and blood dripped on his white t-shirt like ropes of thick honey. I looked around for a weapon... a baseball bat, a hockey stick, anything. But there was nothing.

The zombie apocalypse is not for non-sporty types, I thought to myself. And then... Is this what this is? The apocalypse?

Hoodie flopped around on Silas, jaw snapping. He wanted to get to his face.

"Jeremy, do something!" yelled Silas.

And I brought the laptop down on Hoodie's skull. He tried to stand up and collapsed on the floor next to Silas.

"I'll pay you back for the laptop," I said.

"We need... to get... the hell... out of here," Silas said in between pants.

We ran out of his room, only to be jumped by Pills, whose smile was much, much larger now. Inhumanly large. Most of the skin between his nose and chin had been ripped away. Instead of lips, there were too many teeth and a few strips of meat that jiggled as he walked.

I looked around at our options, and said, "Quick, the elevator!"

"It's really not that reliable," said Silas, "I've been trapped in there twice."

"The stairs?" I asked, forgetting where they were, even though I climbed them just a few hours earlier.

Silas pointed a finger to a door behind the encroaching Pills, who stopped, vomited a spectacular fountain of congealed blood and apple pie, and then continued shuffling toward us.

"The elevator it is," I said.

We ran to the end of the hall to the elevator door, and I tapped the down button about a hundred times. Luckily, it was already on Silas's floor. The doors wheezed open like an asthmatic, and we jumped in with at least a minute to spare.

"Pills isn't a very fast zombie, is he?" I asked.

"Is that what they were?"

But there was no time to answer. Something stirred at our feet, and we both looked down. Our blood froze inside our veins. It was Catnap. We were in such a hurry to get away from Pills, we didn't notice him there.

"Do you think he's..." Silas whispered.

I did not know how Silas meant to end the sentence. Passed out? Asleep? Dead? Undead? So I just said, "Let's not wake him up, and find out."

The elevator dinged. We were only on the 3rd floor. I punched the down button rapidly, but nothing happened.

"Looks like this is our stop," I said.

The doors opened. The hallway was empty. We got out of the elevator and tip-toed toward the stairway at the other end. If we could only get there we would be home free, and then I could call an ambulance, or the police, or the freakin' ghostbusters. I wasn't really sure who yet.

Sneaking out of the House of Bros reminded me of that one time in high school, when I tried to slip out of the house at midnight to visit Craig, my first boyfriend. That felt like the most dangerous thing I would ever do. If I had only known.

"Oh, no. I'm gonna be sick," said Silas, as we moved past an open door. Inside the door lay someone unidentifiable at first glance. Because, you know, it's not that easy to ID a decapitated body, without the head being present and all.

The sticky smell of iron was everywhere.

Suddenly, we heard grunting and groaning from

somewhere ahead of us. We stopped in our tracks, waiting for whatever was making those sounds to show itself.

We didn't linger long.

Hulkules, the massive bunch of muscles with a tiny head, came hobbling out of a room. As he approached us, we couldn't help but stare in amazement at his impressive physique. In his monstrous hand, he held something that caught our attention.

It was a blood splattered pair of glasses, and he was licking at it as if it was an ice cream cone.

"Oh my god," screamed Silas. "The headless bro, it was The Prof!"

I motioned my finger to my mouth to make a 'shhh' sign, but it was way too late. Hulkules already noticed us and was now rampaging in our direction.

This was it. This was how we were going to die. Silas grabbed me around the waist, and whispered in my ear, "I love you."

I giggled into his shoulder. I wanted to say it back, but all of a sudden, we were knocked off our feet. Someone tackled us, and it was not Hulkules, who kept running toward the elevator. Apparently, when zombies get some good momentum going, it's hard for them to stop.

"Hey, Snow White. Hey, Snow White's friend. What did I miss?" asked Catnap. "Man, I feel revitalized! Is there any of that apple pie left? I could go for some pie right about now!"

"Everyone's dead. Some are zombies. End of the world. We need to get out of here, right now, " I summarized.

"And the pie?" asked Catnap.

"Sorry, bro," said Silas, and he touched Catnap's shoulder lightly to console him. "You're better off without the pie, believe me."

Catnap was quiet for a few seconds and then said, "The fire escape will be quicker! Follow me!"

We followed Catnap, who was surprisingly nimble for someone who slept all the time, down the stairs, into his room, and out the window.

We climbed down the emergency ladder, and soon we were home free.

"What now?" Catnap asked.

"Let's head to my car. It's parked two streets from here. Then we can plan our next move."

"Sounds like a plan," said Catnap, and then, "where did Snow White get off to?"

I immediately panicked and started looking around and shouting, "Silas! Silas, where are you?" Then I spotted him walking toward a figure. "Silas, what the hell are you doing?"

"It's Cyrus The Virus!" Silas yelled back at me. "I don't think he's one of them! I think he needs our help!"

Cyrus just stood there, swaying on his checkered Vans.

"You okay, bro?" asked Silas.

"I'm not feeling good, bro. I think there was something wrong with that pie."

"Me too, bro," said Silas.

And then Cyrus the Virus did what he did best. He took three short breaths and then sneezed loudly, directly into Silas's face.

"Bro!" Silas said for the last time, as he wiped the splattered blood and mucus off his face with his bare hands.

---

60 DAYS LATER

I looked at the key card in my hand. I had just swiped it from Doctor Green, and I had to use it quick, before he realized it was missing.

I put my hand up to the glass wall of the quarantine room. Inside Silas, my Snow White, lay in a medically induced coma. That was the best the doctors could do for the infected while they searched for a cure.

But Doctor Green had just broken the news to me. There would be no cure. Most of the specialists were infected. Hope was lost. Sila's glass quarantine room had become a glass coffin.

Silas said he loved me, and I never got a chance to say it back. But actions speak louder than words. That's what my mom always said,

So, I took the stolen key card, opened the glass coffin's door, locked it behind me, and walked over to Silas.

I leaned down, kissed him on the mouth and said, "Don't worry, Snow White, your prince is here."

Epilogue: The Lesson Behind the Story

Love is not measured by how others feel about us. It is measured by how much we are willing to do for those we love. Do you love those closest to you so much that you would battle zombies for them? Do you love them so much that you would become a zombie yourself?

8

The Glass Slipper

Inspired by Cinderella

Why are fairy tales always told from the points of view of princes and princesses? Why not from the points of view of the peasants, the hard-working normal folk? And while we're on the topic, what about the pumpkin carriages and horses? What about the glass slipper? Maybe they have stories to tell as well.

Jeff had always thought glass slippers were severely impractical, and now he was one. Life was a strange old gal, wasn't she?

Before Jeff started his life as one part of a pair of transparent footwear, he was what some would call a career criminal. Or rather, an attempted career criminal. He loved the costumes, the long overcoats, the silly masks, and the sinister hats, but he had been profoundly bad at the actual lying and stealing part.

That's what brought about his current predicament. Having every last left foot in the kingdom violating him, being forced inside his new, reinforced – thank God – glass body. He felt genuine gratitude for every dainty, pedicured foot, and screamed in silent terror every time a fungus-infested size thirteen tried to burrow itself inside him.

Couldn't they see that their potato-shaped toes could not fit inside his petite physique? What a sad joke it was on his part, he thought, that he couldn't speak, but he could still hear, see, feel, and smell! Oh, God, the smells...

At least, he could end it all when he felt he could not take it anymore. The fairy godmother had seen to that. But he was not yet ready to cast the Spell of Kamikaze. Not yet. Just a few more feet.

From the footstool where they placed him, the prince towered above him. He could see right up his royal nose. *Someone needs a trim,* Jeff thought. Under the bushy nostrils, the prince's perfect smile started to lose some of its diplomacy. The unconditional kindness he showed earlier that morning was no longer as non-discriminatory. Jeff could see that it was getting harder, and harder for the prince to fake his warmth.

"Skewer me with a splintery lance," said the prince as a particularly burly peasant reached the front of the line.

You and me both, thought Jeff. *You and me, both.*

"Aren't you the blacksmith?" asked the prince.

"That is correct, Your Highness," said the blacksmith.

"I am most certain I did not dance with you at the ball, Gareth. Do you know how I know that?"

"I think so, Sir. Is it because I am not a beautiful young girl?"

"It is because you are not a beautiful young girl," the prince shouted over Gareth the Blacksmith's answer.

Gareth's face lit up with a pleased expression as he realized he had given the correct answer and raised his lips to form a gummy smile, barely visible through his wild whiskers.

"Then pray tell, Blacksmith, why are you here, wasting my time?"

I would like to know that as well, thought Jeff, and if he still had arms, he would have crossed them. He really missed body language. It really was true: You don't know what you've had till you've lost it.

"Well, the poster here says everyone is welcome to try," Gareth the Blacksmith said. He fished a piece of paper from his pocket and unfolded it like an origami napkin. He held the creased royal notice in his hand for the prince to see.

The prince struggled to keep his impatience in check as he addressed Gareth. "Gareth, now bear with me, do you see that little picture under the words?" he asked through gritted teeth. Although his tone remained civil, his fidgeting fingers betrayed his growing agitation as he waited for Gareth to respond.

"Yes, Your Highness. It's a picture of a beautiful young girl," answered the blacksmith, now smiling so wide you could see his tooth.

"It's a picture of a beautiful young girl," the prince screamed and spots of spittle splashed on Jeff's sole.

Finally, some much needed lubricant, Jeff thought.

The prince held his head in both hands, massaging his temples with long, soft fingers. Everyone in the throne room was quiet. Even the jester in the corner held his hat's little bells tightly in his fists, so they wouldn't jingle.

Finally, the prince looked up again, smiled, and made a 'please continue' gesture with his hand, but Jeff could see what the prince had really meant was, "For God and kingdom, let's just get this shit over with."

What happened next was grisly.

Gareth pulled at his left boot with all his strength until it made a moist sucking sound as it popped off his foot. The ancient sock beneath had what could only be described as a malignant aura.

Jeff was not sure if there was such a thing as the speed of smell or how fast it was if it did exist, but he was sure that Gareth's ghastly sock had just broken the record. Before the boot could even hit the floor, the whole court yowled in unison, "Oooh!"

"Sorry," said Gareth, concealing his smile within his face bristles.

"Please, don't," the prince said when he saw the blacksmith's sausage fingers crawling towards the tip of the sock.

"Gotta finish what I started," said Gareth.

The baker's wife fainted. Fred the unbeliever gave his heart to the Lord and crossed himself. The jester handed out balls of cotton and then plugged his own nose.

Jeff readied himself to cast The Spell. Once he said the magic words, the glass slipper, his body, would melt and he would die. He didn't want to do it. He had come this far. He had smelled the deepest recesses between the foulest toes. He had felt rough warts rub and scratch his insides.

But he was not ready for the abomination of a human appendage about to come toward him. If they had only stayed home last week, like Thomas suggested.

"Or we could go watch a play?" Thomas added an idea to the pile.

But, no. Jeff was in the mood for a heist. He wanted to rob the new shoe store.

"There are some fabulous ruby bedazzled moccasins that would look amazing on you, Tommy," Jeff had said. "And I want to get them for you!"

"So why don't you buy them for me?" Thomas asked, lashes aflutter.

Jeff contorted his face into an expression of deep hurt, and then they both started laughing out loud. Tears streamed from Thomas's eyes as the hilarity of the proposal rippled through his funny bone again and again.

"Imagine that," he yelled, pressing the tip of his forefinger against a tear duct and waving at his face with his free hand.

"So, what do you say?" Jeff asked again, and that time Thomas could not say no.

Alas, the partners in crime did not anticipate the state of the art alarm system of 'Fiona's Footwear'. The complicated rig of pulleys, ropes and bells caught them completely off guard. And soon, before even having had a chance to browse through the summer catalog of mud-friendly sandals – 2 for 1! – they were surrounded, captured and thrown in the dungeon by the king's men. That was the last time Jeff had seen his partner.

Waiting in a grimy cell and contemplating his fate, he heard the lock of the cell rattle. He looked up as an old lady in a vibrant robe and pointy hat entered. She floated toward him, and then sat in front of him with her legs crossed.

"Who… who are you?" Jeff had asked.

"I'm the Fairy Godmother," she said, "and I'm here to punish you."

"Am… am… am I going to… where's Tommy? Did you kill him? Are you… going to kill me?"

"No, young thief. Your punishment will be more… ironic," the Fairy Godmother declared.

And the rest, as they say, was history.

The fairy godmother was not cruel, though. She gave him a way out, and he was planning to use it, but for some reason, he couldn't remember the magic words. *Shit!*

The blacksmith peeled the sock from his foot and it fell to the floor with a wet plop. Something small, moist, and alive escaped from it and ran for its life. Jeff looked upon Gareth the Blacksmith's naked foot in revulsion. He felt bile rise in a throat he knew did not exist anymore.

The foot was corpse white. Its heel was slimy and cracked at the same time, like a mossy mountain range. The toes were too long, and clawed like crab legs. Between them, boggy lichen sprouted in – *quite pretty*, Jeff thought – hues of green and blue. The nails were chipped, yellow daggers. A cloud reminiscent of putrid goat's cheese enveloped the whole scene.

The baker's wife woke up and fell down again. Fred the believer renounced his new god. The jester puked into his bell-riddled hat.

The shock of the tips of the weaponized toenails scratching against his body brought Jeff out of his daze, and suddenly he remembered. He remembered the words!

"Be thy liar, thief or forger,
Love is worth any torture"

He remembered the words, but how was he supposed to say them? He had no mouth! He thought the words again, as loud as possible.

"Be thy liar, thief or forger!
Love is worth any torture!"

Nothing! Nothing happened. And the demonic foot

of the blacksmith was busy forcing his way into him. The yellowed nails screeched as they scratched the glass. This time, Jeff could not only smell and feel it, he could taste the blacksmith's foot juices!

Then he thought of his Tommy. Where was he? What was he? If he was dead, he could be with him very soon. If he could just figure out how to cast the Kamikaze Spell.

He visualized himself and his Tommy, holding hands. Tommy, wearing the ruby moccasins. Both of them were smiling, walking toward a warm, bright light.

And then he gave it one last shot.

"BE THY LIAR, THIEF OR FORGER!
LOVE IS WORTH ANY.."

"Stop," someone yelled at the top of her lungs. It was the voice of a beautiful young girl.

Tears formed in the prince's weary eyes. "It's you! It's you from the ball! You are the one!"

"It is me, my handsome prince! My name is Cinderella!"

"You!" the prince screamed at the blacksmith. "Remove that... thing at the end of your leg from the shoe of my beloved."

The blacksmith did as he was told. The prince picked Jeff up between two fingers and grimaced.

"And you, Jester! Bring an antiseptic potion and clean the glass slipper!" The prince brought his nose close to Jeff and gagged. "The strongest you can find!"

The jester polished Jeff, and he enjoyed every second of it. The last time he'd had a massage was when he stole that couples' spa voucher from Jack and Jill. And he deserved it after the day he'd had.

The glass slipper that was Jeff fit Cinderella perfectly. She and the prince shared a kiss that was, to be honest, a little too graphic for the number of children in the crowd.

Well, that's that then, thought Jeff, feeling bittersweet about the outcome. The story had a happy ending, at least. But as he watched the newly crowned royal couple kiss, Jeff couldn't help but wonder if he would ever have a chance at his own happy ending.

"Your foot looks lovely in that slipper, you know," whispered the prince into Cinderella's ear. "I'll have to get you a new pair. You can't dance with only one shoe!"

"That won't be necessary," replied Cinderella, and she reached deep into her bag.

Jeff couldn't believe what she held in her hand when she took it out. It didn't matter in what shape or form, he would always recognize the love of his life, his best friend, and his partner in crime.

Cinderella put the other glass slipper on her right

foot. And squeezed her feet together.

"I'm ready for another ball!" she said.

"The next one will be our wedding," said the prince.

"I'm so glad you're here with me," said Jeff.

"Me too," said Thomas.

Epilogue: The Lesson Behind the Story

We all do bad things sometimes, and yes, we need to own up to the consequences. But even when all seems lost, and karma keeps sending unmentionable challenges our way, we should never give up hope. A happy ending could be waiting just around the corner, and probably is.

9

The Sacrifice

Inspired by Aztec Folktale

---·◈·---

Aurora is thrust into the midst of a sinister and ancient ritual. The stakes are high, and the odds seem stacked against her. As Aurora grapples with the true meaning of survival and the fragility of life, she is forced to confront the terrifying prospect of being sacrificed for the village. Will she emerge from this ordeal unscathed, or has her fate been sealed already?

Aurora lived in Uthula, a village at the base of the mountain. Their tribe was big and powerful. Their harvest was plentiful, and they had thousands of livestock. All because of the sacrifices the tribe made every year. Or so, they said. A hundred and one livestock were slaughtered every year after harvest. Criminals were thrown off cliffs. Lepers and cripples were driven out. Five virgins were selected by a council of high priests, elders, and the chief to serve in the temple of Siskar. On the last night of the year, the entire village gathered around the temple. Human bones were thrown. The high priest interpreted the signs and called out a name. A name of a girl, young and pure, who is to sacrifice herself for the sake of the village.

Tonight was that night. Aurora was pacing inside her mud house, worried—not about herself but about her kin and her friends. Her mother seemed unbothered. It was as though she believed that would never happen to her daughter.

"Why do you fret, Aurora? The girl chosen by the gods is lucky. She will marry a son of the gods in the next world. Everything denied to her in this world would be paid back a hundredfold." Aurora bit her lip. She didn't think her mother truly believed that. The last time a kin's name was called, blood had drained from her face.

Aurora's father was outside the temple now. She had to convince him to go there. Her father had a peculiar mind, and Aurora was worried she had inherited the same from him. Last year, he had come home incredulously, "I told Miriam's father to run away with his family." He had said to Aurora's mother, "Do you know what he said? He called me a heretic and threatened to tell the village leaders about this."

His wife came at him with her cooking stick. "He should have gone to them," she said, wagging the stick in his face. "You will bring ill fate to this house. If not from the gods, then from the villagers." Aurora had come between them. Her mother cried and cried while her father sat with his head slumped down.

That was a year ago.

This year, Aurora had come of age. She had turned sixteen. Everyone knew what that meant. Her name could be called out. You were not allowed to run away. Nobody did. Aurora had heard of a heretic—a father who had tried to run away to save his daughter. When they were caught, the entire family was trampled on by the herd of oxen. That year was named the year of the ox. And verses were revealed to the high priest.

*"They cannot flee nor conceal,
For the gods must have their fill,
Thus, they must bow to fate's appeal,
And surrender their dear one with will."*

Aurora heard a rap on the door. *It was too soon for Father to come home*, she thought. *Who can that be?* When she opened the door, she found her younger cousin at the door. He was a chubby little kid. He said breathlessly, "Your father … they are fighting … Your name."

She ran past the little boy into the eerie empty streets of her village. She ran past the mud huts, her feet pounding the raw ground and tears flying back from her big round eyes. As she approached the temple, she saw a group of men—priests and soldiers—surrounding a figure on the ground. She ran. When she was a few feet away, someone grabbed her hand and pulled her away from her father. She tried to wrench free, but he was strong. He must have been a soldier. She clamped her teeth on his hand and bit as strongly as he could. Her captor shrieked, and she was free. She saw her father squirming beneath a mountain of a man. His clothes were torn. His face was bloody, but he was alive. Aurora slammed into the man. He didn't budge but laughed out loud. "I think an insect flew into me," he said, and everyone surrounding them laughed.

"Silence!" The word came like a whip, and everyone fell silent. "She is a gift for the gods. Have you no shame?" The men parted, and she saw a tall, dark, blurry figure walking toward her. She wiped her tears with the back of her hand. It was Huascar she saw, and his intense dark eyes were peering into her. "You don't need to force the man down. By gods, you do that enough to your wife." For a moment, both the men stared into each other's eyes. The man sitting on her father's chest spat and got up.

Aurora immediately cradled her father's head. His beautiful face was bruised and swollen. He looked at her with tears streaming down from his eyes. "I am sorry, Child," he said. "The gods are cruel." Feet shuffled around them.

Aurora placed a finger on his mouth. "Let's go home," she said.

They heard the clinking of an anklet coming toward them. "Your mother's here," her father said. Her mother knelt on the ground and kissed him all over his face. Aurora had never seen her show him affection like that. Her mother hugged his face tightly to her bosom. Aurora now saw the woman in her mother. They were man and wife, after all. She had always seen them as Father and Mother. She felt a pang of sorrow in her heart. She will never experience a husband like her father. She will die tomorrow.

"Aurora, Child," her mother said. "Help your father to his feet."

Aurora and her mother helped him to his feet. "You can let go," he said. "I can walk. It is mostly my face."

They walked. Her father limped, and her mother held onto him. The crowd parted before them. The night felt heavy. Aurora thought about her friends. *Were they in the crowds? Were they feeling sorry?* Aurora remembered their talk. They thought the sacrificed girl was lucky. To help her village and to marry the son of a god. Aurora felt anger rise in her. She knew what they would say about her. She knew their words for what they were. Lies. Damn lies. Any woman of age could volunteer to sacrifice herself. She had said so to the girls after hearing their talk. They did not like that. They avoided her for days after that.

Before long, Aurora found herself on her doorstep. A group of soldiers stood nearby, talking and laughing amongst themselves. The family entered their home. The soldiers stayed outside. Her father sat on the bed, his head down and his hands clutching the sheets. He had not talked much. He was thinking.

He got up and hugged Aurora tight. "I will do something. Don't you worry."

"No, Father," she said. "I want you to live."

"How can I live, Child," he said. "The world will be dead without you."

Her mother joined them, and their family cried together. Aurora knew they would come for her at dawn. She savored the moments with her family, looking at their faces and touching their hands. She had never felt so much love inside her heart.

Priestesses came for Aurora right at dawn. Each priestess wore a peplos, a long-draped dress, and a veil over their faces. The chief priestess also had a wig made of long feathers. Usually, they did not wear jewelry, but today, they did. They had anklets and bracelets clinking softly as they moved.

When Aurora stepped out of her house, she saw the entire village standing outside, men in one row and women in another. Aurora walked in the path created by the two rows, led by the order of priestesses. Men and women threw petals of flowers at her. She had fantasized about walking to the temple, flanked by men and women, as a bride. But this was different. It was supposed to be her father that led her.

She looked at her clothes. They were the ones she wore yesterday. She could see her father's blood on them. The blood reminded her of last night. Numbness turned to fear. She feared for her father. He was too intelligent for his own good. He believed he could solve everything. "*Do not accept your fate. Accept your past,*" he would say to her. She knew he was bound to try something.

When he was young, he had been captured as a prisoner of war by the city beyond the mountain. He had run away from there, climbing their walls, as tall as mountains, escaping hundreds of city guards, and prowling the walls, clad in shiny armor. He had come home with gold in his pocket and a smile.

Aurora was only three years old then. She had never met him. Aurora was suspicious of him at first, but he quickly won her over. And since then, it was always Aurora and her father against her mother, teasing, playing, and talking.

One night, when they lay on the ground gazing at the stars, her father had admitted to her that he liked the city beyond the wall, which he called Palmyra. He would not have returned if not for Aurora and her mother. Her father had said that the people there offered the gods sheep and goats instead of young girls. And their gods were more powerful for sustaining a city that large. The city had paved roads. The houses were built with blocks of rocks so strong that you could stack one house over another. The houses were painted white, which kept them cool in summer;

they claimed. Food was plentiful. Every day, dozens of people came to the city to exchange their food for a round piece of metal called a coin. Everyone worked for coins. You could exchange anything with them. There were places that served food and drinks in exchange for the coin.

The temple of Siskar stood tall and wide in the morning gray light. Its walls were made of baked mud bricks, and its roof was thatched. The ground around the temple was kept empty for congregations. Before Aurora even reached the temple's doorstep, she smelled the woody sweet smell of incense. Inside the temple, the light was dim, and the air was smoky. The mud floor was even and cool. The walls were etched with drawings of warriors, priests, and chiefs from the past. A small fire burned at the foot of each deity: the creator, the sustainer, and the destroyer.

Each of these deities had hundreds of incarnations. Kaltar the merciless was one of the incarnations of the sustainer deity, Nuraya the nurturer. It was said that when Kaltar was being created by Nuraya, a whiff from the destroyer, Dufkur's clothes got to Nuraya's and tainted Kaltar, which made him merciless. Without sacrifice, Kaltar holds the sustainment from the villagers, and some even say Kaltar sabotages the harvest by rain or pests.

Aurora heard the silent sound of water coming from the back that mingled with the sounds of playing children. One of the priestesses led her to the other end of the temple. The mountain was right there at the boundary of the backyard. In the center of the yard was a round pool of hot water under a tree with pale limbs and red leaves, which made the tree look as if it was on fire. A silent breeze passed through the backyard, and out of the congregation of leaves, a single solitary leaf fell into the pool. Aurora shivered.

Aurora was bathed, dressed, and adorned with jewelry in front of the deities to stand as a witness. She was led outside, and she stood at the top of the steps. She could see everyone from up here. It was incredible how two feet in height can change the view of the world. She thought about her father. About how he had changed from living in the city, he called Palmyra.

The crowd was scattered. When they saw her, they moved closer to the temple. Aurora knew everyone. Her little fat cousin was standing in the front. Her unrelenting uncle stood aloof. She saw her young friends standing in a group together. They forced a smile when they saw her. Aurora saw her mother pushing to the front. *Where is Father*, she thought.

The high priest, the chief, and the elders stood to her right. The high priest was a short portly man. He had come to the village from Palmyra, a young man, asking for refuge from the devils in the city. He had helped the tribe broker peace with the city, making the city pay half of the grains the tribe used. That had won the entire tribe over. Before, they had to raid caravans going into the city for food. And because of him, they were given food in exchange for nothing. But Aurora's father had said it was a lie. The high priest was no magician or deity. In Palmyra, the old people who knew him called him a swindler. One old man said he was part of the negotiations between the tribe and the city. It was decided that the city would pay the tribes in grain if they promised to not attack their caravan. The attacks were ruining the city's reputation and affecting trade. Aurora's mother did not believe her husband. She had come at him for spewing blasphemy of the city devils. Aurora's father had said he did not believe them until he saw the high priest in the city's pleasure houses.

The high priest stood beside Aurora on the steps, and he smelled like lavender and powder. He spread his two hands and said:

"My dear brother and sister in faith, we gather here together in the presence of gods and men to witness a feat of the sacrifice made by not only her parents but also by the whole tribe, for god is our witness. In our hearts, we love this young child as much as we love our own children, as much as we love our nephews, and as much we love our nieces. This is a moment of incredible sadness for her family, evident by the events of last night, and for the tribe, and for many of you that came last night to bear witness to the honesty of her old man. She is ready to embark on a journey to the top of the holy mountain behind me. She will be accompanied by the greatest warrior as decided by the council. For the eighth time, the longest in history, Huascar will accompany her and sacrifice her to the gods."

Huascar came riding on a horse with a group of soldiers. The crowd parted and gave way. He dismounted, looking at her. Aurora looked away. He was almost as tall as her while she stood on the steps. He came close to the priest and said, "Are you done?"

"My father. Have you seen my father?" asked Aurora to Huascar.

"I have not, but it is almost time. We must leave at sunrise."

At that, Aurora saw her father. He came striding towards her, still limping a little from his injuries. He had a huge gash on his forehead, but he looked fine. Tears fell down from her eyes, and she couldn't help but run towards him and hug him. "Please don't do anything, Father," she said.

"I won't," said he as he stuffed something in her

belt. He kissed her on the cheek, and they separated. The first light of morning fell on her face. *Am I really going to die tomorrow morning?* It was hard to believe. Everyone she loved was with her. It all seemed like a dream until suddenly, she saw Huascar walk towards her. And he lifted her like a sack of flowers on his shoulders. The world was upside down. He turned around and strode towards the base of the hill. Everyone followed. Children chased them. They were jumping, trying to touch her hair. She was embarrassed. *Is this how I am going to part ways with my family? By being carried like vegetables?* She lifted her upside-down head, and her face flushed. She saw her father limping towards her, with concern on his face, but he was not crying. Thank the gods for that. He was not crying.

Huascar followed the downtrodden path up the mountain. The slope was pretty steep. She felt like she would fall any minute, bouncing up and down on his shoulder. When they were pretty far up, he put her down on her two feet. After that, she walked. The trail was narrow and winding. As they traveled higher, the air grew cooler. And the trees were sparser. They hiked in silence save for the crunch beneath their feet and their labored breathing.

After hours of walking, they stopped for a rest under a tree and watched the sun go down as the wind massaged their long hairs. Aurora was grateful for the view. She was grateful for the feeling of being alive. She was grateful for the cool air. And weirdly, she was grateful for a companion even though he happened to be her butcher. She thought about her father. *What is he doing?* And her poor mother.

"We need to move," said Huascar without looking at her. "There is a cave. We can sleep there without freezing to death."

Aurora became aware of how cold it had gotten, with the sun setting and them being far up the mountain. It was hard to breathe there. They resumed their journey. Her leg ached as it had never before. *Must I die with cramps in my leg?* Her feet felt heavy and sore. Her jewelry scratched and clawed at her. She felt dizzy and hungry. Huascar must have seen her because he told her to climb on his back. She tied her hands around his neck, and he grabbed her legs. She felt like a little kid. She could smell the sesame oil on Huascar's hair mingled with his sweat.

She watched the moon come up gradually. She had always wondered how it came gradually as the sun does or in an instant like a thunderstorm. The sounds of the night came with the moon. The insects chirped and buzzed around them. Wolves howled some distance away.

They were well into the night when they reached the cave. The cave was tucked away in the side of the mountain, its entrance hidden behind a thick curtain of bush. When she moved past the foliage, Aurora saw dry wood at the mouth of the cave and sleeping straws inside its belly.

At first, her mind went to mountain bandits, but she realized that was silly. It was probably for the two of them so that they could rest at night. Aurora made herself comfortable on the straw bed. Huascar lit a fire with his knife. And the cave was filled with light and warmth. Aurora was hungry and tired. Her whole body ached. She put her feet against the fire and felt good.

Huascar sat at the mouth of the cave. Shadows of flame flickered on his face. He looked as old as her father, but she knew he was younger. *It is those scars,* she thought. Thinking of her father, she remembered something. Her father had put something in her belt. She carefully reached down to it, her eyes never leaving Huascar. He was hooked into his thoughts. She felt a small glass vial. She took it out. She knew it was poison. It must be. Or it could be a sleeping drought. It was more likely to be the latter because she knew her. Aurora tried to think of how she could feed him this liquid. Maybe she could slip it into the food. *The water skin!*

Aurora asked Huascar for water. He threw the water

skin to her. She caught it, fumbling. She pulled the cork out and drank to her fill. It was a long journey to transverse. Aurora felt scared. It made no sense. Even if she got caught, the outcome would be the same. She slipped the liquid into the bottle with a shaky hand while keeping an eye on the ruthless warrior. Her whole body was trembling. Huascar turned towards her. Aurora was sweating. Her hands were clammy. She said, "I need to go relieve myself."

"Looks like it," he said with a sly smile. "Go before you pass out."

She stood and quickly strode out of the cave. The warmth turned to coolness. The cold air on her sweaty body made her feel like she would freeze to death.

"Don't go far," she heard Huascar shout at her. She found a bush to the right of the cave and relieved herself. She felt better. She straightened her dress, took a few deep breaths, and walked back.

Huascar sat with his back to the cave, eating dried meat. As she walked back, his eyes followed her. They made her feel guilty. She moved past him into the cave. The water skin was lying on the straws.

Before she could sit down, Huascar said, "Pass me the water skin," with a mouth full of dried meat. Her heart was beating fast. She bent down, picked it up, and handed him the skin. She went and sat down on the straws. She pretended to stare into the fire but kept peeking at him.

He pulled the cork out. Aurora's heart was pounding inside her. He lifted the waterskin to his mouth. Aurora was intently looking at him. His mouth touched the skin. But before he drank it, Aurora saw his eyes look sideways. Her heart felt as if it would blow out of her chest. Huascar smiled.

He knows. She thought. She might have gotten scared, but she steadied herself and gritted her teeth. Huascar had put the water skin down and was studying her face. She looked at him defiantly.

"What was it?" he asked, "Poison?"

"A sleeping draught," she said.

"How generous of you," he said and chuckled. "Do you think it's the first time this has happened? The last girl tried to poison me."

She knew whom he was talking about. Her father had a spat with Aurora's father.

"You will be surprised …" said Huascar. "many of these young girls don't want to die. I guess it is not much of a surprise. Two of them tried to stab me. One of them had a brother hiding in the cave waiting for me. Some did not have the courage to do anything, but they begged and cried."

Aurora sat with her head down.

"He is a good man, you know. Your father," Huascar

continued, "I looked up to him. I was a new boy in the army. He would stick up for recruits. Great Marksman. Best I ever saw. He was captured soon after I was made a soldier."

Aurora was listening intently. "How did you know about the sleeping drought?"

"I know your father. He does not believe in our gods and our rituals. He had confronted me seven years ago, after my first sacrifice. He said I was a good boy and tried to convince me to commit a sacrilege. I denied. Last night, when your name was called, I knew he would do something. He is a brave man. I kept an eye on him. But I did not see him slip anything on you. He is too slick, I guess, even for me. But you were not as slick. I only had to peek to see your trembling hands pouring the draught into the water skin. You should sleep. Tomorrow will be a long journey for you."

Huascar closed his eyes and went to sleep. *Does his mind ever sleep?* thought Aurora. *Can I run away from him?* She did not think so. She closed her eyes and was surprised at how easily sleep came to her. *Does it feel like this? Death,* she thought to herself. In her dreams, she saw her father and the city beyond the mountain. A shadow. A shadow came and rescued her. It was a tall shadow. Strong and muscular.

Huascar woke her up at dawn. She sat inside the cave, looking out. The horizon had turned red. She saw blue hills and misty mountains far ahead. *Do all gods need sacrifices?* she thought. *Are they aware of the suffering of this world? Or don't they know what it is? They must have never experienced it because if they did know, how could they be so cruel? How could they take children away from their mothers, brothers from their sisters, and food from tables? Have they ever felt hungry? Ever scared as I am now?* Aurora did not think so. *But then, men murder other men, children, and brothers. They steal, rape, and pillage. But do they ever truly understand others' suffering except when they experience it? Did I ever truly understand all the women that were sacrificed before me? Could men truly understand the loss of someone else's? Memories are etched on the sand. They wash away as time flies by. What remains are faded scars. But what are scars compared to wounds?* Yes, thought Aurora. *Gods do not get wounded or get scarred. Men have scars. And women too. Deeper. But no one has wounds except the wounded.*

Huascar was sitting on a piece of rock, looking at her as she thought. When she looked, he asked politely, "Can we go now?"

Aurora stood up and untangled her dress. She plucked out the pieces of straws that stuck to it. She felt the cool fresh air on her face when she walked out of the cave. Birds chirped, and she felt moisture in the air. She heard a distant gong coming from the west. She looked as if she would see a bell in the sky.

"It is coming from Palmyra. They do that every day. To wake everyone up," said Huascar looking towards the west.

"What if someone does not wake up?" asked Aurora.

"They do nothing. It is simply a tradition, a ritual, like our rituals," said Huascar.

"Like 'our' rituals?"

"Like 'most' of our rituals," said Huascar as he stood up.

The slope was steeper near the top. The shrubs were sparser. Aurora felt coarse gravel beneath her feet. The wind was strong. She tried hiding behind the Huascar's massive body as they climbed, but the wind sneaked up on her. It was getting hard to breathe. Dirt flew into her mouth when she opened her mouth to breathe. She brought her right forearm before her eyes as her eyes wept due to the dry wind and the fine gravel. She looked up, squinting. Huascar climbed crouching, with his long hair flying behind him.

Aurora remembered what her father had once told her. "If you are dying, it is best to remind yourself of the worst parts of life. And when you are not, it is best to remind yourself of the good parts of life." Aurora's mother had chided him for talking about death with her. Aurora had agreed. She did not want to talk or think about death. Thoughts of death would sneak into her mind, but she would quickly change her thoughts or actions so that she may live in illusion. But as she climbed, death stared into her eyes. And this time, it was not sneaking. It held her and forced her to look him in the eye.

The wind suddenly went still, or it lessened to a degree that Aurora could not feel it at all. She lowered her arm and opened her eyes. They had reached the summit. It was not as narrow as it looked from the base. It was as big as the temple below. In the center, two rocky outgrowths jutted out of the ground. A huge eagle sat at the top of one of them. *That's the actual summit*, thought Aurora.

Huascar grabbed her hand and led her across to the other side. Aurora saw the city beyond the wall. It was magnificent. A perfect circle embedded in rolling green hills. The grass dancing in the wind from afar gave the illusion of the sea. Aurora felt as if she was stranded on an island. She saw the ship in front of Huascar. Right there. A magnificent circular vessel. *Would they hear if I waved my hands*, she thought. *Would they come and save me?*

"It is a good city," said Huascar, peering down. "Not the best I have been to, but it would do well."

"Do well for what?" asked Aurora, gazing towards Huascar and squinting in the morning sun.

Huascar looked towards her and smiled, with his hair blowing in the wind. His face shone with the golden morning sunlight. Aurora saw a twinkle she had never seen before in his eyes. Of course, she had not. She had never looked. His face was young. His smile was sweet yet sad.

"You are free to go," he said, squinting in the morning sun.

"I do not believe you," she said smilingly, but she did believe him. There was no way those eyes were lying.

"Did you spare everybody?" asked Aurora.

"Except the old ones."

"But there were no—" Aurora stopped midway, realizing her foolishness.

Aurora heard a whoosh. A groan escaped Huascar's mouth as he fell to one knee.

Aurora looked back and saw her father with an arrow pulled tight in a bow. He limped towards them, his face still black and blue from the bruises. "Father, don't shoot."

"Get away from him, Aurora," he said.

"First, put down your bow, Father," said Aurora as she shielded Huascar. "He is not going to kill me."

Aurora's father hesitatingly pulled his bow down.

"He does not kill any girl, Father. He lets them escape

to the city."

Aurora's father put the bow down on the ground and limped towards Huascar. Together, Aurora and her father hauled his massive body under the shade of the jutting rocks. Her father laid out his cloak and placed Huascar's bag on it. They rolled him on his back, over on the cloak. The arrow had pierced the calves.

Aurora's father pulled out a knife and cut Huascar's pants. He poured some water from his water skin. He gave the knife to Aurora to cut off a piece of cloth from her dress and handed it to her father. "Now, hold on tight. Put your weight on it."

"I am going to pull the arrow out," he said to Huascar. When he pulled it out, Huascar let out a muffled groan. He poured some more water and tied the cloth tightly around the wound.

"You will need to get the wound burned and cleaned when you go down," said Aurora's father as he helped Huascar sit. "I only meant to injure you so that Aurora could escape. If you told me you were going to let her go, I wouldn't have come."

"You think I should tell every father every year, and they won't find out. Worse yet, until some fanatic tells on me."

"You could have told me. You knew me."

"I could not risk it," he said, then he turned towards Aurora, "You should go."

"What if they ask how you got wounded?"

"Don't worry about that. I will get down in the middle of the night and ride straight out of the village to our camp near the river."

"How will you get down?" she asked.

"Your father will help me. We will first sear the wound when we reach the cave. After a night's rest, I should be able to walk on it. Now, haul me up, you two."

Aurora and her father helped Huascar up and took him to the edge of the mountain. "Go down carefully. And when you reach the city, they will take you in. They know why you are here, but they will not feed you. Look for Ayar's house, and you will find other girls there. He will feed you, but you will have to work. I will come to see you soon. After some time has passed by, I will bring your father with me. But keep your ears open. Do not let anyone from the tribe see you. You will be wearing their clothes and braiding your hair their way, so you will be hard to identify, but be wary."

"Thank you, Huascar," she said and then stood on her toes to kiss him on his cheeks. Aurora hugged her father, who was trying to hold it together. And then, she carefully started descending the mountain. When she looked back, they waved at her and smiled.

Epilogue: The Lesson Behind the Story

Beliefs have the power to either lift us up or hold us back. Blindly following them can lead us into dangerous waters. Therefore, we must question traditions and remain mindful of our beliefs, instead of blindly conforming. We hold within us the power to create our own path and choose our destiny, rather than meekly following the herd. But to do so, we need to summon our inner resilience, determination, and courage, and stand up for ourselves in the face of adversity.

10

Bad Influence

Inspired by King Midas

---·◈·---

When a mysterious organization gives Midas Kingsley, a caring veterinarian, the opportunity to change his life completely, he cannot say no. But he will soon realize, nothing comes for free. For him and his daughter, fame and fortune will come at a price worse than death.

In the reception area of the animal hospital, Midas Kingsley handed the kitten back to the itchy woman.

"Add this to the back of Delilah's neck, and those fleas will be gone before you can say 'infestation,'" said Midas as he smiled warmly and gently patted the woman's hand to reassure her.

"Thank you very much, Doctor," said the lady, scratching one red knee. "Does one call vets, doctors?"

"Yes, Mrs. Parsley. We are called doctors. We went to medical school and everything."

"But not a real one, surely? Probably a tiny school for pets?"

"Let me know how it goes with the fleas, Mrs. Parsley!" said Midas, and he shut the front door in her face before she had a chance to say another word.

"I'm so sorry, Lilly! That woman wouldn't shut up. And that poor little kitten…"

"It's almost 6 p.m., Dad," said Lilly, "I have homework I need to do on my laptop. I'll never finish in time now." She scooped up her mathematics books, stationery, and calculator from the waiting room's plastic seats, and transferred the jumbled bundle into her backpack.

"I'm really, really sorry."

"Let's just go, please."

In the car ride home, Lilly asked Midas the same question she always asked him, and like always, he hated it.

"So, Dad." She looked at him, brows furrowed and arms folded. "How many of God's creatures did you murder today?"

She never asks him how many pets he had saved, only how many he had had to put down.

"Only two today." He had put down thousands of pets in his career, if not more. And he despised it.

"Only two?"

"Only two." It had been six.

"Why can't you do something else? Like, something where you don't have to take innocent lives?"

Midas furrowed his brow and tilted his head slightly in a quizzical manner as he looked at his daughter. "Like what?" What was this child on about? Ever since her mother had passed away, she had become stubborn and excessively opinionated. He did not know how to connect to her anymore. But something in Lilly's words rang true. *I would love to get a bit more appreciation*, he thought to himself.

He observed her laying with her cheek pressed against the BMW's window, her breath creating small patches of vapor on the glass as she spoke. "Do you know what Caitlin's dad does for a living?" she asked.

"Caitlin Evanson's father? Craig? Isn't he a mechanic?" *Good grief child*, he thought, *you want your old man to fix cars? How is that better?*

"Used to be a mechanic. Now he's an influencer. He makes like thousands of dollars a week. Sometimes a day."

Midas looked at his daughter with eyes like saucers. "No! What? Craig's an influencer? How does that even work?" Craig wasn't exactly the sharpest syringe in the med kit.

She just shrugged and mumbled. "I dunno." With a stiff finger, she drew a large dollar sign in the remnants of her breath on the window.

When they arrived home, Lilly went to her room to do the rest of her homework. Or try to, anyway. Just as she sat down by her laptop, her dad's phone rang. Shortly after, she heard muffled yelling through the closed door. She jumped, opened it, and screamed down the stairs, "Dad! What gives? I'm trying to pass my year over here!"

"Missus Parsley, Missus Parsley, please calm down," her dad continued. Then there was silence, followed by a loud crash. Although she was not in the room, she recognized the sound of a phone hitting the wall.

She went downstairs to see what was wrong with her dad and found him in the living room, on the floor, face buried in his palms. She hoped he wasn't crying.

She approached him cautiously and placed a hand on his shoulder. He looked up at her and began gesturing wildly with his hands.

"You heard what I said, right? I told that woman to put the medicine on the back of her cat's neck. You heard me right? What does she do? She drizzles it over the poor little thing's food," he exclaimed, his voice rising with each sentence.

He was beside himself, so Lilly sat down next to him and put her scrawny arm around his wide back. "It's OK dad. It'll be OK." His face stayed firmly fixed against his palms. "Did the little girl make it?"

Then he looked up, tears streaming from his dark green eyes. And then she knew. Delilah, the kitten, didn't make it. He then stood up, retreated to his bedroom, and shut the door quietly without saying goodnight.

As he retreated to his room, Lilly sat there feeling helpless and uncertain of what to do next.

"I'm so over this!" Midas screamed into his pillow like a frustrated teenager. "Somebody help me! Anybody!" Lilly had been right. It was time to make a change.

He sat down behind his computer and typed a query into the search engine:

HOW. TO. BECOME. AN. INFLUENCER.

He scratched his stubbly chin for a while and then added:

OVERNIGHT PLEASE.

Then, he pressed search. He waited. And waited. Nothing happened. He tried to press the search button again, but lo and behold, the mouse pointer would not move. His piece of crap computer had frozen. He reached for his phone, but it wasn't there. It lay in fragments on the living room carpet. He probably shouldn't have done that.

He switched the computer off at the wall socket and climbed into bed in his work clothes. They were still covered in tiny black hairs of Delilah the kitten.

The following morning, Lilly plopped down next to him on the bed to wake him up. She whispered in his ear, "No fair, Dad! No fair!"

He jolted awake. "What, who, where? What did I do?" She handed him the package, already opened.

"I've been begging you for months to buy me a new phone! And in a matter of hours after yours breaks, *ding dong*, special delivery!"

He rubbed the crumbly sleep from his eyes and squinted at the brand new phone on his nightstand, his brow furrowing in confusion. "Lilly, did I drink last night? I don't remember ordering this," he asked, his voice laced with a hint of frustration. His gaze flicked over to the computer on his desk, which was still unplugged from the wall.

"I don't know what you do in the privacy of your own room." She smirked and left the room. "Enjoy your new phone, you big fat hypocrite!"

"I'm not fat," he tried to yell after her, but it came out as a pathetic whisper. His full attention was fixed on the box in his hands. Had he won a competition or something?

Later, after charging the phone for a full six hours – because that's just what dads do – he switched it on. He turned the phone's empty packaging around and around in his hands. It was strange. No logo. No brand name. Nothing. The phone was also plain black with no identifying marks.

The loading circle stopped spinning and a message filled the screen:

'Would you like to quit your job? YES or NO?

He squinted suspiciously at the words. "What the hell," he thought out loud. He squinted some more, pouted his lips, and then tapped *yes*.

'Would you like to become an influencer?'

He was now thoroughly bewildered, but he tapped *yes* again.

'Do you agree to the terms and conditions?'

He couldn't see any terms and conditions anywhere, and he wasn't in the mood to look for any either, so he tapped *yes* again.

The sound of a cheering crowd erupted from the phone and a new, longer message appeared:

'Welcome to your new life, Midas.
Everything is about to change.
What you hold in your hand is the future of influence,
A tool that will make you famous overnight.
I heard your call, and I have provided.
All your social profiles have been set up,
And everything you need to continue is on the phone.
Yours Truly
Lucy Fir Incorporated

"Damn, modern technology is something else," he said to himself. He had no idea what had just happened, or how. All he knew was that he was excited for the first time in a long time. He had a chance to get respect. To stop killing pets. To make real money. And most importantly, to impress his daughter.

A new message popped up:
'Take your first photo and let's post it.'

No time like the present, he thought, and started swiping and tapping wildly on the phone. Before he could figure out exactly how the gadget worked, he heard the antique sound of a lens snapping. A new message appeared:

'First photo posted! Congrats, Midas!'

Under the message was the photo he had taken. A blurry shot of his feet.

"Oh, come on, really?" He exclaimed, feeling exasperated. Realizing he needed Lilly's help to sort out the situation, he headed towards her room. As he approached her door and lifted his hand to knock, a 'bloob' sound emanated from the phone, drawing his attention to the new message he had received:

'10,000 *likes*, 8,000 *subscribers achieved!*
Keep doing what you're doing, Midas!'

It had to be a joke, he thought, but then notifications for comments on his photo started streaming in at an unfathomable speed.

'Amazing!'
'Now that's art!'
'Wow!'
'Why didn't I think of that?'
'Be my baby daddy!'
'So inspiring!'

Midas' world was spinning. He was overwhelmed

with anxiety and confusion, mixed with a hundred other emotions. But above all, he felt like he was on top of the world.

As the days passed, Midas posted photos of everyday stuff; his feelings, dad jokes, and basically anything he wanted to. And every single post was a hit. A week later, he had over a million followers, and he could not keep up with the notifications.

Lilly watched in awe. She couldn't understand why people loved her dad's posts so much, but she didn't care. Midas' success made her happy. One day, she asked him, "Dad, you must be making tons of cash now. Can I get a new phone and maybe a new laptop?"

Midas chuckled. "Money? Oh yes, money. Those flat and round things. Pfft... Of course, I'm earning a lot. Piles of the stuff." In truth, he wasn't making any money yet, and had no idea how to go about it.

He went up to his bedroom, planning to find out how he could convert his followers to cash. He had the reach. It was time to monetize. The thought hadn't even completely formed in his mind when the phone rang. That had never happened before. He put it to his ear and answered with warily.

"Hello?"

"Midas Kingsley?" asked the man on the other side. He spoke in the hurried, matter-of-fact voice of a narrator in a 1950s radio commercial. Before Midas could answer, the caller continued, "What am I saying? Of course it's you! It has come to our attention that you would like to monetize, monetize, monetize! Well, Midas, today is your lucky day. We're offering you a one-time only chance to turn each and every follower you have accumulated, and will accumulate, into one dollar!"

Midas was stunned. That's a lot of dollars.

He didn't know what to say next. He stumbled over his words and finally said, "How?"

"We thought you'd never ask, Midas! We're going to send you a post. All you have to do is press confirm to make it public. That's all!"

"I don't understand..." he told the wacky caller, but the line was already dead.

He held the phone an arm's length away, and looked at it as if he was seeing it for the first time. Who and what was this? As he considered the phone, the promised post popped up. It was a photo of Missus Parsley watering her garden. Underneath was a caption:

'Remove Mrs. Jessica Parsley from the City Council immediately. Here she is watering her garden! And we're in the middle of the worst drought in centuries. Let's cancel her!"

Midas had not forgotten how she killed her kitten. So, without any hesitation, he tapped on the *confirm* button, and seconds later he received a payment confirmation. $124,111,000 had been deposited in his account.

The next few days, he kept doing what he had been doing, but he was getting bored of it. He wondered if he could make even more money if he put some thought into it. Lilly, by this stage, had received a new phone, laptop, wardrobe, and a complete makeover for her room. He had even given her a credit card linked to his account. So Midas asked her for help with some posts. It was the least she could do.

"I can't, Dad! Got a party tonight," she said and rushed out of the house.

"Ok, then," he said absentmindedly and posted a photo of the kettle.

Likes and new followers were still abundantly easy to rope in; like shooting fish in a barrel.

That next morning, the sound of his phone ringing jolted him awake. At first he thought it must be the good people at Lucy Fir Incorporated calling him with another offer. Who else would call at three in the morning? But it wasn't them. It was the police.

Midas Kingsley didn't even get out of his pyjamas. He just grabbed the closest pair of shoes, ran to his car and rushed to the police station.

"Is she okay? Is my little girl okay?" he asked the first police officer he saw as he entered the precinct.

"Please, have a seat Mr. Kingsley," said the police officer. His hair was salt and pepper, in a style that was still stuck in the '70s. His eyes were dark and deeply creased around the edges. He pulled a chair up so it faced Midas, and then he sat down. Midas could smell coffee on his breath. Maybe something stronger.

"Mr. Kingsley, " he continued, "your daughter is in a shitload of trouble."

"Lilly? What did she do?"

"Do you know where your daughter was last night? Well, earlier this morning, actually?

"Lilly was at a party, but she wouldn't do anything bad. What did she do?"

"She was at a party, yes. One hundred good dad points for you, Mr. Kingsley. But the exact location of the party is the problem. It was at the McMillan's. You know them, right?"

Midas knew them very well. He used to treat their two pugs, Miley and Cyrus. The McMillans were great pet owners, but they were not nice people. They used to take months to pay their bills, even though they were loaded. They were beyond powerful. In fact, they owned most of the town.

"What about them?"

"Their house burned down. And the rest of the kids are saying your daughter did it."

"How? I don't understand. Where's Lilly, is she hurt?"

"Apparently, she was trying to light fireworks in the house as a prank. For social media or something. Anyhoo, the fireworks lit up some cashmere curtains, and soon the whole house was in flames."

The police officer leaned in closer. Now Midas was sure he had had something extra with his coffee.

"We can make it go away, Mr. Kingsley."

"Go away?"

Between his knees, where only himself and Midas could see it, the police officer rubbed his thumb and forefinger together.

"The McMillans have insurance, so that will cover the damage to their home. But it won't cover the emotional stress and trauma of losing their beloved pets, Miley and Cyrus. They were so badly burned the family was hardly able to identify them. What type of dogs were they? I couldn't make out."

Midas gulped down tears. "Pugs."

Midas followed the policeman to the nearest ATM without working cameras. Obviously, he had done this before. He asked Midas to raise his daily limit and withdraw all of his money, and Midas didn't care.

He could make more money. What was at stake now

was his daughter's safety, and their reputation. What if this got out and he was canceled? He wouldn't be able to make money online anymore, or go back to being a veterinarian. Those poor little pugs. He just wanted to pay the officer and get it over with so he could erase those charred little bodies from his mind.

Balance: $0.00

The text appeared on the ATM's screen. How was that possible? Did Lilly do this? Had she emptied his account? What had become of his sweet, exemplary daughter?

He showed the balance to the policeman, whose expression suddenly changed from cocky to brooding. His fingers absentmindedly tickled the butt of his gun.

"No need for that," said Midas, "I'll have more money tomorrow. I promise!"

The policeman started sliding the gun out of its holster.

"A million dollars! I'll give you a million dollars tomorrow!"

The officer hesitated for a moment before reluctantly agreeing. Before Midas even reached his house, his phone rang

"Please, please, help me! The police have my daughter! I need money quickly," he yelled into the telephone, not even sure who it was on the other side.

"Midas Kingsley! Would you like to make a million

buckaroos tonight? If your answer is yes, please approve the post we have prepared for you! It's for a petition to push through a new law. Nothing serious. Your social influence will help make it happen. It will change millions of lives!"

Midas pulled the car over and immediately started fingering the phone's screen. It was a no-brainer. He approved the post without even looking at it.

A FEW DAYS LATER

Everything was back to normal in the Kingsley household. Midas stopped answering calls from Lucy Fir Incorporated. He realized he had been a bad influence on his daughter. He was a vet again, but he no longer worked from an office. He traveled to people's homes to treat their pets. That way he knew almost for certain they were safe from their idiotic pet owners.

And Lilly? Well, it looked like she had learned her lesson. Who wouldn't after a debacle like that? She was sitting next to him on the couch, eating macaroni and cheese, when the news bulletin interrupted the show they were watching, "Pets From Hell."

"Boring," said Lilly. She looked at her phone. "Got a call! Need to take this." She left the room.

A pretty blonde newsreader, who looked as if she had been crying, spoke.

"Breaking news. A new bill rendering pet ownership illegal was passed today. Those against the passing of the new law were clearly in the lead until renowned overnight influencer, Midas Kingsley, tipped the boat by signing a petition declaring that because people cannot look after their pets, they should not have them."

Midas's jaw hung on the floor.

"Please call the no-more-pets hotline to schedule your pets' euthanasia."

Midas turned off the television. What had he done?

From the other room, he heard his daughter speak to someone on her phone.

"Yes! Sure, I'd like to make a million dollars," she exclaimed.

Epilogue: The Lesson Behind the Story

Hopelessness and anger at our current situations can be catalysts for change. Sometimes we just need that little nudge to open ourselves up for new opportunities, but we must always be vigilant to how the changes in ourselves might affect those around us. Remember, we are all influencers, and bad ways are transferable, even without intent.

11

A Taste for Teeth

Inspired by The Tooth Fairy

---⬦---

*T*he world would be a magical place if fairy folk really existed, wouldn't it? Imagine how they could improve our lives! If humanity and fairies lived and worked together, the world would be an enchanting wonderland. But what if our two worlds fused, and fairies were not as helpful and benign as the tales told us they were?

Casey screams like a banshee, but the big bunnies on either side of her don't even flinch. The bunny on her left is baby blue, the one on her right, a light pink. Both of their mouths are frozen in gigantic toothy grins, and their eyes are glassy. Most of the creatures of the new realm serve the Tooth Fairy, whether they want to or not.

The limousine hits a speed bump hard enough for Casey to bounce and hit her head against the leather door panels.

"Ouch!" she exclaims.

"Sorry about that." says a solemn voice from the front passenger seat. It belongs to Whiskers, a giant striped field mouse, dressed in a sleek black power suit.

Between bouts of tapping on her tablet and screeching instructions into her headset in field mouse language, Whiskers tries to answer Casey's questions.

"Where are you taking me?" asks Casey.

"I think you already know the answer to that question, Love," says Whiskers.

"Not to the Tooth Fairy, please!"

"I'm afraid it is so."

"But, why? I don't understand! I have a disease. And I have a doctor's letter to prove it."

Casey runs her hand over her pockets, searching for the familiar feel of the folded envelope, but she can't find it.

"Looking for this?" asks Whiskers, holding a piece of paper between two manicured claws.

"Please don't. I need that!" Casey whimpers.

Whiskers unfolds the piece of paper and reads.

"To whom it may concern. This letter confirms that Casey Carmichael suffers from ankylosis and is thereby exempt from paying tooth taxes to the Fairy Kingdom. From the office of Doctor Beagleson."

"See," Casey screams. "I told you! Now please, let me go."

Whiskers looks deep into Casey's eyes, crumples up the letter, and throws it out the window.

"No!" yells Casey, and starts crying.

"Tell me more about this disease you have, Casey. This... ankylosis. What does it mean?"

Casey wipes her eyes and her nose on her sleeve, and speaks between sobs, "It means my baby teeth have fused to my jawbone. It means I don't have to pay tooth tax, because my teeth won't fall out by normal means."

"Not by normal means..." says Whiskers with a hideous grin.

"It's in the Tooth Fairy's constitution! Only teeth that have been lost by natural means need to be paid to her majesty, the Tooth Fairy!"

"My dear," says Whiskers, "I regret to inform you, but the rules have changed."

Only now does Casey notice what's in the blue bunny's fluffy paw. A massive claw hammer.

She feels a sting in her right arm, and has just enough time to notice a long syringe in the pink bunny's hand before everything goes black.

When she wakes up again, she is surrounded by darkness. She blinks her eyes once, twice, just to make sure they are actually open and that she is not still dreaming. She blinks for the third time. *Dammit*, she thinks. She is awake.

She tries to move, one limb at a time, but to no avail. She feels tight straps biting into her wrists and ankles.

Casey wonders what happened to the Tooth Fairy. She used to be good. When the fairy folk took over the human realm last year, everything changed for the better. The Tooth Fairy, who took on the role of queen, stopped wars, famine, climate change, and other calamities that humans had unleashed upon Earth.

The fairy folk supply the humans with food and meaningful work, and in return the Tooth Fairy only asks for their children's baby teeth. What she does with the baby teeth is a mystery. But, it is said that in the fairy realm children's teeth are a symbol and source of purity, and the Tooth Fairy needs the teeth to keep the realms stable.

But recently, it seems, things have changed.

All of a sudden, Casey hears a buzzing noise, and then she's engulfed in flickering fluorescent lights. She scrunches her eyes, and surveys the room.

Leaning against the farthest wall, is the big blue bunny. Next to him is a large framed portrait of a beautiful fairy, with long curling black hair, oval eyes, a friendly smile, and a pair of glistening wings. It's the Tooth Fairy, and she is magnificent.

Whiskers, assistant to the queen, stands by the door, arms folded.

"Welcome back, sleepyhead,"

"Where am I?" asks Casey, and forces tears from her eyes. She doesn't need Whiskers to answer her. She knows exactly where she is. She is exactly where she wants to be.

"You are in the operating room, my darling. It's time to loosen those toothsies!"

"No!" says Casey, faking panic.

"Would you like anesthetic?"

"Yes?"

"I'm just pulling your leg Casey. We're all out of anesthetic!" says Whiskers, and giggles.

"Please, you don't have to do this!"

"Oh, but we do."

"I've heard the rumors!" says Casey. "The rumors

about your queen. That she's treating you badly! It's true, isn't it? She's become addicted to adult teeth and it's changed her. She's turned into a monster!"

"It doesn't matter," Whiskers hisses. "She's still our queen,"

"She doesn't have to be. You know what the Fairy Folk's Constitution says. The person who kills her will become the new ruler! That can be you Whiskers!"

"No, I…"

"We'll help you! Right, blue bunny? Together, we can overpower her! Kill her with that hammer. Become the new queen and make things right again!"

Whiskers and the blue bunny are silent for a while. At first it seems they are contemplating it, but then Whiskers snarls. "Blasphemy! For that, you will die! We don't need you alive to extract your teeth!"

Whiskers then grabs the hammer from the blue bunny's paw and moves toward Casey.

Well, it was worth a try, she thinks. Whiskers raises the hammer with the clawed side down, ready to bash Casey's brains out, but is interrupted by a loud gurgly voice.

"Stop at once! She is mine," says the voice. It sounds like the person behind it is speaking with a mouth full of chunky vomit. Every word sounds difficult and painful.

"I'm sorry, Your Majesty, please forgive me," mur-

murs Whiskers, and sulking, moves to the corner of the operating room.

"Your Majesty, " Casey says with mock-respect and grimaces at the thing.

The monster that used to be the beautiful Tooth Fairy is now a big, gray tumor-looking blob with tendrils and fangs growing out of it at weird angles. Its eyes are a dull yellow. Its wings, black and veiny. And what used to be a smiling red-lipped mouth is now a gaping maw with teeth like stalactites.

"I've tasted all types of teeth. All the flavors. From the molars of greedy politicians, to the incisors of murderers, and the canines of lying lawyers. But you, my dear, have something special! Something I haven't had the pleasure of sampling yet," says the monstrosity that used to be the queen.

Casey gulps loudly. She knows what comes next. She prepared for it, but, she still doesn't want it to happen. The pain...

The Tooth Fairy continues her soliloquy. "This disease you have. Dental Ankylosis. It makes my mouth water! Your teeth are a delicacy. Somewhere between the sweet enamel of an innocent baby and the fruity stink of a hag's rotting roots. The combination is... exquisite."

"Thanks," says Casey, and adds a sob at the end. She

forgot to sound sad for a moment there.

Saliva drips from the hole that was once the fairy's mouth, "I can't wait any longer! Whiskers, give me that hammer," screams the Tooth Fairy.

Suddenly, the blue bunny is behind Casey, and she feels four hooks slip into her mouth. Two hooks lift up her top lip, and another two stretch her bottom lip down toward her chin.

This is going to hurt, she thinks. But it's for the good of humankind, so she will endure.

Without warning, the gray, gurgling thing with the ragged teeth starts bashing at Casey's mouth with the hammer. First with the blunt side, then with the claws, now with the blunt side again.

The pain is worse than anything Casey could have imagined. Colors she has never seen before flash in front of her. Teeth and blood splatter in all directions and sting her eyes. With every impact of the hammer, she either passes out or regains consciousness. Seconds feel like hours. Minutes, like millennia. Warm iron streams down her throat, and she coughs it up. Red drenches the Tooth Fairy's face, but she just licks it off with a phlegmy black tongue.

Finally, the bludgeoning stops and she drifts into sweet, sweet oblivion.

A few minutes later, a sickly crunching sound wakes

Casey up. Her mouth is a swollen mess. Her head feels as though it's been trampled by an angry rhinoceros over and over.

"What are you eating?" she tries to ask. "Are you eating my teeth?"

The Tooth Fairy does not answer. She – it — is in a trance.

That's when Casey starts to laugh. It hurts so much, but she can't help it. She guffaws with delight. Blood and pieces of her tattered lips hit the walls.

Casey's laughter seems to somehow capture the Tooth Fairy's attention, as she looks at her with glazed and confused eyes, but continues munching away on Casey's special teeth. And then it starts. It begins with a slight bubbling under the gray skin of the Tooth Fairy, and then the bubbling turns into large quivering bumps. The Tooth Fairy expands like an ugly balloon.

When Casey visited the doctor to get a new certificate for her dental disease, he gave her some bad news: She is dying. Apart from the disease that caused her teeth to fuse to her jaw, she also has oral cancer.

After months of grieving and depression, she woke up one morning and came to a realization. Her cancer isn't a curse. It can be a gift. A gift for all humankind.

"What. Is. Happening?" the Tooth Fairy screams as she grows and grows, like a thirsty leech sucking blood.

And then there's a loud pop, and what remains of the queen slides down the walls and drips in slimy ropes from the operation room's ceiling.

Casey's eyes close, and she slips into darkness again. Perhaps for the last time. But from far away, she hears someone scream. Is that Whiskers?

"Quick, get the fairy dust! We have to save her. Our new queen is dying!"

Epilogue: The Lesson Behind the Story

Everything is good in moderation. The problem is knowing when to stop. We regularly hear about pop stars, influencers, actors and people from all walks of life who were once saints, but were changed by bad habits. Addiction makes people forget who they were and can make monsters of anyone. Especially the best of us.

12

The Alchemist's Android

Inspired by Rumpelstiltskin

---◈---

Mistaken for an android, Autumn is thrown into a prison of broken things where she meets a mysterious new friend. How long can she survive and give the king what he wants before they discover her secret?

It was a mild summer's day in the kingdom when the door of Gregory Cuff's house blew off its hinges. Butterflies rested on the chipped roof as three burly guards burst into the foyer. Gregory could hear bluebirds singing sweet melodies in the cool, pine-scented air outside as the largest of the three guards grabbed him by the neck and threw him against a wall, hard enough for two taxidermy deer heads to come loose and clatter to the oak floors.

"It's time to pay up, Cuff!" growled the guard.

Gregory was not unprepared. He was expecting this.

Not many people know this, but in every kingdom there is only enough space for one great ruling force at a time. Back in the day, when Gregory was still a spritely young elf, the kingdom and all its natural and unnatural laws had been governed by one such force: magic. And in the times of magic, Gregory had been the proprietor of a booming alchemy business, Goldfingers, where he turned everyday objects into pure gold.

But nothing is forever, as Gregory had soon realized. A few weeks ago, magic was suddenly dethroned by a new ruling force. Everyone saw it coming, but no one could have predicted how abrupt the change would be.

Magic had not fizzled out. It didn't evaporate over

time. It was just, all of a sudden, not there anymore. Erased out of existence. Gregory's empire of alchemy toppled overnight. He could no longer turn objects into gold for money, but that wasn't the worst of it

Soon, outraged ex-customers began knocking on his door. All their precious things that he had previously transformed began reverting back to their former pre-gold forms; Pots, shoes, rocks, bottles, a baby's first diaper, and even expired pets and loved ones. Golden statues commemorating those who have passed on turned smelly and much less shiny. There was a lot of shouting.

The coming of the hyper-tech age changed everything for Gregory.

"The king's crown has turned to wood, and he would like to know how you plan to rectify the situation," continued the pug-faced guard with a voice like rolling thunder.

Gregory smiled his best the-customer-is-always-right-smile he could muster.

"I'm glad you came! I've actually got a gift for the king. Autumn! Where are you? Come say hello to the king's nice people!"

A barefoot, golden haired elfish girl in a plain white dress emerged from a dim corridor and joined them in the doorless foyer.

"This is Autumn," said Gregory. "My gift to the king."

"The king has enough concubines, Cuff. He needs you to fix his crown!" said the guard, and he moved in to grab Gregory by the throat.

Gregory dodged the darting arm and cowered on the floor. "No, please! Wait! She isn't blood and bone! She's only created in the image of an elfish girl. She's an android."

All three guards crossed their arms and scrutinized Autumn.

"It looks really lifelike," the one with the eyepatch said.

"The king has all the androids he could wish for. What would he want with this scrawny thing?" asked the fat one.

On the inside, Gregory chuckled at the irony of the situation. The king, who had had all the gold he could wish for, had launched an attack on the tech realm of Silikonia, slaughtered its whole population, and taken every gadget and piece of tech he could find as his spoils. This unnatural shift of forces is what caused the death of magic, the hyper-quick takeover of tech, and consequently, the disappearance of all the king's gold. *What a moron*, Gregory thought.

"His Grace, the most-wise King Dornus, would certainly have a use for an android that can transform objects into gold, would he not?" The words dripped from Gregory's mouth like wild honey.

The big ugly one thought it over for a few seconds and then said, "Okay, but if it doesn't work, we'll be coming for a head."

As the three guards walked away, escorting Gregory's only daughter to the palace, he packed a suitcase and spoke to himself. "Good riddance, good for nothing. And now to get far, far away from here."

In the darkness of the storeroom of the palace, Rumplestiltskin sat holding the cold hand of his dead life partner, Stipperoomp, who had been badly damaged in the king's raid on Silikonia. Her circuits were fried, her memory drives obliterated. In the end, Rumplestiltskin had to put her out of her misery. He had to switch off the love of his life.

And now, he had decided, he could not live without her anymore. His nimble, mechanical fingers moved to the pop-out touch panel on his torso, and he started typing the password that would commence his self-destruct sequence.

But before he could finish typing the last letter, a sudden wave of light illuminated the room. Something flew in and landed on the stone floor like a sack of turnips.

Sad whimpers escaped from the heap on the floor. It was crying.

"You'll find plenty of things to turn into gold in here," said a guard, "I'll be back tomorrow morning to monitor your progress."

He slammed the door shut, and belly-deep laughter echoed through the halls outside the storeroom.

Inside the storeroom, the crying continued.

Rumplestiltskin removed his fingers from his control panel and glanced toward the sobbing thing using his night-vision. Maybe I should try to cheer her up, he thought.

"Turning things into gold! That's a very nice talent. You know, a friend of mine used to be able to do that," he said, stroking Stipperoomp's cheek.

"I can't turn anything into gold! I'm not even an android! I'm an elf!" said Autumn.

"Oh, that's what they all say, my dear. Poor thing. Your master probably told you that you were flesh and blood. Well, I'm sorry to break it to you. Most of us had to go through that realization at some time in our pseudo-lives. We're nothing more than circuitry and algorithms."

"I don't have a master! I have a father. And he hates me. Because of what happened…"

"Come now, I'll sort this out in a jiffy. I'm going to take an X-ray of your insides and aircast it to you, and then you'll see what you are. Don't worry, it won't hurt."

While Autumn continued lamenting, Rumplestiltskin fired up his X-ray vision and took a closer look at what made Autumn tick.

"Oh my," he said.

"I know," she said, wiping her eyes and nose on her dirty sleeve.

"You're pregnant."

Rumplestiltskin's artificial synapses sparked excitedly inside his metal head. There were so many new possibilities now. He had a new potential friend. This pregnant girl. No, that's not right! He had two possible new friends, if he counted the unborn baby. But wait! What if the king found out about the baby? Then they would know this girl was not an android, and they would surely kill her. And on that note, she might be killed even quicker if they found out she couldn't do gold transformation.

He felt the processes running in his head come to a satisfying halt. It was going to be the hardest thing he's ever done, but he had a plan.

That night, he opened up his loved one like a cadaver on a slab, and carefully took out all the special parts that made her the technological marvel she used to be. He then carefully implanted the parts into himself, closed them both back up, and got to work.

When Autumn woke up the next morning, she felt something cold and smooth in her hand.

"What, what's this?" she asked, disoriented.

"It's a golden gear. I made it for you."

"You made it for me? How?"

"Don't worry about that. When the guards come later, you give that to them."

Loud steps reverberated outside the door, and a key turned in a lock.

"Thank you! How can I repay you?" Autumn asked.

"Don't worry about that now, just do as I said," he whispered.

Autumn did as she was told, and the guard was impressed.

"So, does that mean I can leave?" Autumn asked the guard.

The guard laughed in genuine amusement. "What? Are you crazy? You're going to stay here forever!" He threw the wooden circle, which previously was the king's crown, at her. "Tomorrow morning, that better be a solid gold crown," said the guard, "or else."

He dragged a finger across his throat.

Rumplestiltskin explained his plan to Autumn.

"Those are my conditions, and in return, I will continue transforming objects into gold for the king."

"You want my baby? And you want to, what? Turn him into a thing like you?"

"He'll live forever, and he'll still have a soul. Don't you think I have a soul?"

"I don't know, " she said.

"This is your only option, Autumn. Otherwise, they will kill you and your unborn daughter!"

"It's a... She's a girl?"

"Yes, you have a healthy baby girl growing inside you. Please, let me do this."

"What if the baby dies during the... operation?"

"Then you can kill me. It's easy. Just say my name three times. Rumplestiltskin. That will trigger my self-destruct function."

"Okay, Rumplestiltskin. Please save my daughter."

Days became weeks, and weeks became months, and Rumplestiltskin kept to his word. Every day when the guards opened the door to the storeroom, Autumn was ready to deliver the day's requested gold.

So far, Autumn had been able to hide her pregnancy from the guards by covering herself with silk blankets and tarps she – or Rumpelstiltskin – was slowly but surely transforming into golden duvets for the king.

Soon, enough months had passed for Rumplestiltskin to perform the operation. Autumn was reluctant, but not about to go back on her promise. She allowed him to put her under using special vibration-based anesthetic.

"Count to ten," he said.

Before she could reach number four, her body fell into oblivion and she was out.

It is widely known that the elven mind could only be stretched so far. It was rigged with fail-safes and special ways to make sense of unnatural, foreign input. This made elves resilient and adaptable. But the thing that Rumplestiltstkin cradled in his arms was beyond the processing capabilities of Autumn's fragile mind.

She did not know exactly what she expected, but it was not this. She assumed her daughter would have skin. If not like hers, at least the synthetic kind that covered Rumplestilkstkin's mechanical body. But this... thing... was... naked.

It was a mix of wires and organs and pipes, blood vessels and lights and eyes. It had limbs, but they were attached so bizarrely that her baby girl – or this abomination – looked more like a squashed insect than her daughter.

Autumn screamed. And screamed. She screamed for the guards and for the king, for her father, and for Rumplestiltskin to please kill it. Please just kill it.

She did not care what happened next. She would come clean. She would tell the king that she was human. That she could not transform his things into gold. She would tell him that it was all Rumplestiltskin. And then, finally, they could kill her. And she would be free at last.

"Stop screaming," Rumplestiltskin whispered. "You don't understand what you're doing!"

But she paid him no mind. She kept on yelling and screaming, until she felt as though she would throw up her lungs.

Eventually, the guard arrived.

"What's all the noise about? Some people are trying to sleep through their shifts here," said the guard.

Autumn, who was now bashing her body against the walls, screamed at the guard, "I'm not an android, I'm an elf! Please take me to the king!"

"The damn thing has lost it," said the guard. "Alright, alright, let's go before you break yourself."

But before they reached the kings' chambers, Autumn saw herself in a large mirror that hung on the hall for the first time in months.

She did not recognize the thing she saw.

Where was her hair? Her pointed ears? Her skin. She

was gold and shiny, and her eyes protruded from holes in metal. When she rotated her neck, she could see wires coiled around her spine. She could see her spine!

"Oh, are you coming to your senses now?" said the guard, gripping on to her hard, mechanical arm. "See there? That's you! You're a machine."

"No! It can't be!" she uttered. Her final sentence. Something broke inside her. Maybe something mechanical, or maybe it was just her heart.

"C'mon, young lady. Back to your cage."

The thing that used to be Autumn sat slumped somewhere in the darkness of the storeroom.

"I'm sorry Autumn," said Rumplestiltskin. "It was for your own good. I had to make some alterations. Come be with me! Be my wife! Be a mother to our child. We'll be happy here. Together forever!"

Autumn tried to say the password. She wanted him to explode. And she wanted to explode with him. Rumplestiltskin. Rumplestiltskin. Rumplestilskin.

But she was broken, and no words would come out.

Epilogue: The Lesson Behind the Story

Be careful who you trust. Many people will enter and leave your life. Although some may look like they have your best interests at heart – and some of them might – be careful that they aren't only looking out for themselves. Always make sure there is balance in all your relationships, that what's given to you is worth what's taken from you.

Pure Damn Beautiful Sorcery

An afterword by the author

Tattoos are like stories. Or at least, they're supposed to be – I'm looking at you Uncle Tom with your Chinese symbol for 'Prosperity' that actually means 'Pork fried rice'.

So let me rephrase, tattoos are *sometimes* like stories, but I believe stories are always like tattoos.

They cling to our souls and snap into place. They are newly discovered puzzle pieces, fragments of ourselves that we never even knew were missing. The only real differences between stories and tattoos are that stories are living things – and cannot be lasered off.

Why do we draw on our bodies with permanent ink? To rebel against the man? To alter our outside so it more closely resembles what's inside us? Perhaps. But I think the real reason we turn ourselves into works of art is to add twists to our own tales. We want to show the world – or sometimes just ourselves – that there is more to us. We are not all the same. Look closer, if you dare!

We are 60% water and 40% stories. (Can't argue with science, baby!)

Stories are a big 'ol chunk of who we are. But what makes stories even more amazing is that they change according to time, place, mood and even other stories they have to share their space with inside our spongy brains. The stories we read – literally! – change us. *And I don't care if I used 'literally' wrong here, that's how I feel about it, so deal with it editors!*

Reading *Lord of the Flies* later in life and having read it in school are two completely different experiences, and essentially two different stories, although on paper, it's the same. Add *Moby Dick* to the mix, and the context changes again. Sprinkle in a bit of *The Great Gatsby* and just a dash of *The Hobbit*. Now you've got a party going! Each story you read builds on the ones you have already read. They find ways to hug, mesh and twist together in fantastical ways.

Stories, whether they are fairy tales or great American novels, are modern day magic. Never forget that. The act of placing one's thoughts on paper and then projecting those thoughts into uncountable hungry minds across the world is not commonplace. It's pure damn beautiful sorcery. It's sharing secrets with a novelist who crafted boundless worlds on a notepad in her car, it's impossible collaborations with dead dudes from hundreds of years ago, and it's experiencing thousands of lives without leaving your home.

Stories have a mystical power to transport us to other worlds, to let us experience the impossible, and to make us understand that we are part of something greater than ourselves.

And I'm going to tell you a secret now, so listen closely. We are the custodians of stories. We are their caretakers. Even the most boring stories were once poignant, and bursting with meaning, but time takes its toll. Meaning does not disappear, it simply becomes 'every day'. Like if you eat sushi everyday of your life – it loses its magic. (And oh lordy, is it magical!)

It's up to us to keep things fresh, try different recipes, get things in a twist. Add some ghost peppers to your california rolls, why don't you!

Endless possibilities tingle at the ends of our fingers like a wonderful itch.

Don't just crack open a book and read – although that's a good start! – go forth and fight the war on the mundane. Create your own twisty paths, walk them and create magnificent maps, so others can follow you into the brilliant dark.

Wow, you made it to the end!

If you enjoyed this book, would you be against leaving a **Good Review on Amazon**?

As an up-and-coming author, your feedback is incredibly valuable as it provides the opportunity to continue improving and deliver even more captivating stories to you. Plus, it'll give us a chance to connect. Win-win, right?

Thank you for sticking with me through the twists and turns of these fantastically twisted stories. I can't wait to share more content with you soon!

Ava May is an up-and-coming writer driven by a deep love for literature. Growing up as an orphan, she found solace in the magical worlds of Dickens, Doyle, Austen, and classic fairy tales, sparking her passion for storytelling from a young age.

Blending modern twists with classic themes, Ava is passionate about bringing stories that have shaped our culture to a new generation of readers. Her writing aims to bridge the gap between generations, reigniting a love for timeless tales that are filled with wisdom and lessons from the past.

Residing in London, Ava spends her days writing with the company of her loyal feline friend, Hemmingway. With a heart full of passion and a dedication to storytelling, she is an author to watch in the world of literature.

H ey, before you go, I want to remind you not to forget about your free stories!

I've curated a collection of some of my all-time favorite unpublished tales, and they're waiting for you in the **FREE eBook**.

So be sure to check them out and enjoy some extra reading. And don't worry, there's plenty more where those came from.

Scan the QR code to claim your FREE eBook!

Printed in Great Britain
by Amazon

46272142R00118